MW01659535

Halloween Heist

Smart Money

Stuart Cannold

Copyright © 2025 Stuart Cannold

All Rights Reserved

ISBN:

DEDICATION

This book is dedicated to all who wear the uniform. Without you, the USA would not be the free country it is. Thank you for your service.

To my wife who gave up her time to help with this process, and kept me somewhat sane, although she will argue that I wasn't wrapped too tight from the gun.

Enjoy Halloween Heist: Smart Money.

Jonah:
Enjoy Heist.
Thank you.

ABOUT TONY

My career with the LAPD spanned over 20 years. I was an unseasoned rookie fresh out of the academy in the fifties. I could write a book about my experiences as a cop. Fortunately, I was a better cop than a writer.

Police work during my tenure wasn't the joke it is today. You could handle criminals in ways that you can't now. There weren't cameras affixed to every building. There weren't cameras on cell phones—hell, there weren't even cell phones yet. Body cameras hadn't been invented. And the news? It was reported the way it should be—honestly, without slant, and with the facts.

But that's getting ahead of the game. Let's go back to the seventies in the San Fernando Valley. Let me share one of my stories with you...

6:05 P.M.

THE CALL COMES IN (SGT. ANDERSON)

Sgt. Anderson answered the phone at 8:05.

"Yes, sir. Yes... Yes, I can hear you fine... Yes. Okay... Yes. I understand."

The sergeant took a breath. "Your name?"

He scrawled something on a half sheet of paper. "Will you tell me where you're calling from?"

The sergeant made another notation on the paper. As he did, there was a sharp click. The connection had been broken. The phone was dead. He stared at the receiver for a moment, then hung up. He hesitated only briefly before pressing the button that buzzed his boss's office.

An off-duty patrolman was sipping black coffee from a container. "What's up?"

"The usual." The sergeant's tone was matter-of-fact. "Some asshole claims he's taken over a theater and is holding people hostage."

"Jesus," the off-duty cop said. "Which theater?"

The desk sergeant shook his head. "Dunno. He said he'd call back in about ten minutes.

12:05 P.M.

PLANNING THE HEIST (THE CREW)

Early that afternoon, five men sat in the back booth of the Derby Deli Restaurant, directly across from the Mountain Theater. All of them shared a common goal. In just eight hours, they would be putting their lives on the line—gambling everything for a chance at two million dollars in cash.

09:07 P.M.

FIRST CONTACT (THE LIEUTENANT)

"Well, spit it out, sergeant," the lieutenant ordered.

"I got a call," the sergeant said, "about two or three minutes ago. It's probably a prank. You know how Halloween is."

The lieutenant interrupted. "Sergeant... the facts. Now."

The sergeant sighed. "Yes, sir. This guy called," he began. "He said he's taken over a theater and is holding people hostage. He wouldn't give his name, and he wouldn't tell me which theater."

The lieutenant nodded as if he had the complete picture. "Could it have been a kid?"

The sergeant shook his head. "No, I don't think so. He said he'd call back in ten minutes." He glanced at his watch. "That would be in another seven or eight minutes. I assume he'll have more details then."

"You assume, sergeant?"

"Yes, sir."

"Would you like to explain that?"

The sergeant cleared his throat. "I'm sure it's a prank. I mean, who the hell would be stupid enough to try something like that? That's suicide. You couldn't get away with it. Even if you did get the money, how the hell would you get out? Impossible. Couldn't be done."

The lieutenant smiled. "Let's hope you're right, Sergeant. I'd hate to spend Halloween trying to get some punk out of a packed theater."

"Yes, sir."

"I've got to admit, though, it would be unique. Can you imagine," the lieutenant mused, "taking over a theater filled with people?"

The sergeant shook his head. "No, sir," he said sarcastically. "I can't imagine that."

The lieutenant was no longer smiling. "I'll be in my office if he calls. Buzz me immediately."

He turned and walked toward his office.

Meanwhile, Tony Dangerfield's wife, Nancy, lay in Mac's arms on the bear rug in front of the fireplace. She was completely relaxed—she always was when she was with Mac. With him, she was at peace with the world.

"Hey," Mac whispered, brushing his lips lightly against her ear. "Don't fall asleep." Glancing at his lieutenant's buckle, he added with a smirk, "I don't think I'm quite ready for sleep."

If Nancy heard him, her only response was a hint of a smile. She reached for his hand and brought it to her lips, gently running her fingers between his. When she felt Mac's muscles begin to tighten, she took his finger between her teeth and teased its tip with her tongue.

Mac sighed, knowing what was coming. He loved it—every

teasing, playful minute of it. Every passion-filled second... He squeezed his eyes shut. There had to be some way he could work things out...

Nancy gazed into Mac's soft, sad brown eyes. Her own blue eyes, alive with mischief, sparkled as she smiled. She pushed him down onto the bear rug, cradling his head so that it rested gently against the bear's. Once she was sure he was comfortable, she climbed on top of him.

TONY DANGERFIELD

Tony Dangerfield isn't just another Valley cop. He leads a highly trained team of half a dozen men, assigned to special cases—cases that require a different kind of approach. A different kind of cop. For this reason, the men called themselves simply the STOP SQUAD—a special team of police.

Dangerfield was chosen to lead the squad because he had conceived the idea. He sifted through hundreds of men until he found exactly what he was looking for. Then, he began to shape and mold them.

He started with a handful of what he called "raw cops"—all experienced veterans. But for Dangerfield's purposes, it was still raw.

He ran them through his own academy—an intensive, twenty-two-week program that he personally designed. The handful of men who endured the training swore it was rougher than the Special Forces' preparation during the war. Dangerfield gave them a choice: if they couldn't handle it, they could return to their original assignments. Only one man dropped out.

After twenty-two weeks, Tony had built something more than just a team—he had forged a brotherhood. A group of men so highly trained, so close, so in sync that they jokingly referred to themselves as the Machine.

Nobody came before the Machine. Not wives. Not families.

Not girlfriends.

When TD said, "Jump," the Machine asked, "How high?"

8:17 P.M.

THE DEMANDS (THE VOICE)

At precisely 8:17, Desk Sgt. Anderson picked up the phone at West Valley Station. Instantly, he recognized the voice. Without hesitation, he buzzed the Chief.

"Sgt. Anderson," the voice on the other end said. "Just listen. I'll do the talking. Ask your questions when I'm finished."

The voice was slow, deliberate.

"I'm fully aware that everything I say is being recorded. It doesn't matter. I want you and anyone else listening to fully understand the situation. I estimate we have between four and five hundred people in this theater—men, women, and children.

Before you panic, understand this perfectly: Nobody... I repeat... nobody will be hurt if you meet our demands. Furthermore, Sergeant, at this very moment, the press, radio, and television are being notified."

Anderson clenched the receiver tightly.

"Let me explain further. We are not a terrorist organization. We are highly organized and highly trained. Some of us have killed before. In other words, Sergeant, we are not afraid of killing again. I hope I'm making myself clear.

I told you—our intention is to hurt no one. I mean it. All we want is money.

To prove this isn't a prank, we are inside the Mountain Theater at Victory and Topanga. I suggest you confirm that this is not some Halloween joke. Dispatch a car now, while I'm talking to you, and have them check it out.

Once you're convinced I'm serious, we can proceed."

The voice paused.

"I'll hang on, Sergeant. Do whatever it is you do to get the car in motion."

Anderson shot a glance at his superior, then quickly dispatched a unit.

As the call continued, Chief Parker walked over to the front desk, took the phone from Anderson, and spoke directly to the receiver.

"This is Chief Parker. Who is this?"

The voice on the line chuckled.

"Chief, don't give me any of your bullshit. All you're doing is wasting time. And in this case, time isn't just money—it's lives. Do I make myself clear?"

Parker hesitated only an instant. "You make yourself clear. Go on."

"As I was telling your sergeant, we are holding between four and five hundred people—men, women, and children—hostage in the Mountain Theater. While we're talking, he's verifying my claim.

Our intent is not to hurt anyone. We want money. When our

demands are met, every person in the theater walks out alive.

But if anything gets screwed up, you'll have only yourselves to blame.

Play by our rules, and everyone lives happily ever after.

Mess with the bull, Chief... and you'll get the horns.

Comprende?"

The Chief took a deep breath. "I understand."

"Then check your watch. What time do you have?"

Parker glanced at his wrist. "8:23."

"Good," the voice said. "The show is scheduled to let out at 12:05. By then, we will have in our possession—delivered by someone of our choosing—two million dollars in cash.

If that money is not here, on time, there'll be a late show, Chief. Do you get me?"

Parker's grip on the receiver tightened.

"On your shoulders, Chief, rest between four and five hundred lives. Do you have any questions?"

The Chief took about fifteen seconds to gather his thoughts. It was useless.

"No, I have no questions."

"Fine. Then whatever you need to do to get that money together, I suggest you get started.

Oh, and before I hang up, let me add this—we have

automatic weapons. Machine guns.

Need I say more?

Two million dollars. By midnight. No games.

I'll call back in half an hour to check on your progress."

There was a sharp click. The line went dead.

Parker took a moment to light a cigarette. He inhaled deeply, then exhaled, his mind racing. Finally, he turned to the sergeant.

"Get me, Tony Dangerfield. Tell him I want him in my office immediately. Top priority.

And after you've gotten hold of Dangerfield, get me a print of that voice recording.

I want it on my desk when he gets here."

8: 45 P.M.

PANIC IN THE PROJECTION ROOM (SID HIGHLAND)

Theatre manager Sid Highland sat on the floor of his office, his shoulders barely touching the wall. His hands were tightly bound behind his back, and his feet were secured with thin nylon rope.

Sid glanced quickly at the other employees. They seemed calmer now, not as close to hysteria as he was.

He cursed himself. He had to get a grip. He couldn't lose control.

Maybe he'd wake up. Maybe this was all just a dream. Maybe it wasn't really happening.

Maybe he'd hear the alarm. Then, Louise would gently shake him awake, and he'd be back in the safety of reality.

Sid laughed, but the sound was hollow. It had to be a dream. A nightmare. Who'd be crazy enough to take over a theater? The thought was ludicrous. Ridiculous. Preposterous.

But then, Sid suddenly stopped laughing. The rope was cutting into his wrists.

8: 50 P.M.

DANGERFIELD JOINS THE CASE

Tony Dangerfield stormed into his boss's office. He was big, strong, and rough—just the way he liked it. But tonight, he was also pissed off. His evening had been interrupted, and he wasn't happy about it.

The cigar he placed in the Chief's ashtray was unlit.

"What's up?" Dangerfield growled.

"Sit down," the Chief said. "This may take a while."

One look at the Chief, and Tony knew something was very wrong.

"Okay," Tony said, sitting down. "This better be good. You didn't pull me away from a piece of ass, but you did drag me out of a good poker game."

Tony fired up the cigar, blowing clouds of thick, white smoke toward the ceiling as he puffed, waiting for the Chief to speak.

"Tony, this one is a bitch. A real mother."

Tony leaned the cigar on the lip of the metal ashtray. "Sounds like a major crisis."

The Chief raised his eyebrows, his forehead furrowed with worry. "It may be worse than that." He paused. "How familiar are you with the Mountain Theater in Woodland Hills?"

"You mean the one across from the shopping center?"

"Yeah."

"I've taken my wife there a few times. We've also shopped in the center. I don't know it like the back of my hand, but I'm familiar with it."

Tony's mind raced as he tried to anticipate the Chief's next words. What the hell was he getting at?

"Is the problem in the West Valley?"

"The problem is in the theater. There are about five hundred people in that theater, Tony. They're being held hostage."

Tony whistled. "Jesus H. Christ. You've got to be kidding!"

The Chief shook his head. "It's no joke, Tony."

"Who in his right mind," Tony asked, "would pull something like that? Are you sure it's not just a Halloween prank?"

The Chief shook his head. "It's been checked out, Tony."

Tony rubbed his fingers and thumb over the stubble of his beard. "Give me the details."

"I'll do better than that. We've got the voice recordings. Everything's on tape."

"How much do they want?"

"Two million."

Tony whistled.

"Do we know how many there are?"

The Chief shook his head. "All I know for certain is that

they've demanded two million dollars, and we've got until midnight to come up with it."

The Chief stopped the recorder after Tony had listened to it for the third time. "That's unbelievable."

"Get philosophical later," the Chief said. "We've got work to do."

"Have you talked with anyone else inside the theater?"

"I haven't made a move," the Chief said.

"How many people know about this?"

"If you want to believe our friends in the theater... probably half the world. They said they were notifying the radio, press, and TV."

Tony drummed his fingers on the desk. "They haven't missed a trick. One thing's for sure. We're not dealing with a bunch of amateurs." He reached for his cigar.

Tony puffed thoughtfully on the cigar, finally working up the nerve to ask. "Chief. You're not going to pay them, are you?"

"You know my thinking. I'm concerned with the victims. I'll do anything I can to ensure their safety."

"There's another school of thought," Tony said. "You should consider."

"What's that?"

"If you pay these pricks, you're opening a door."

"And if we don't," the Chief said, "are you prepared to bury the victims?"

Of course, Tony cared for the victims. But at that moment, his mind was racing ahead. There were other things to consider—like the possibility of getting inside the theater—and a million other questions he needed answers to.

"Well?" the Chief finally asked. "Any ideas?"

"What about the owner?"

"We're still trying to locate him. He's out partying."

"Well, when we locate him, see if he can come up with a floor plan. That might help. And while we're at it," Tony added, "let's see if we can get hold of the company that did the air conditioning job."

Tony was deep in thought as the Chief barked orders into the intercom.

"You know," Tony said when the Chief stopped talking. "We've got other problems. There are a couple of bars close to that theater. A restaurant and an amusement park. There's a 24-hour gas station across the street, a Sears service center on the northeast corner, a B. of A., and a deli on the southwest corner..."

"What's the point?" the Chief asked impatiently.

"The point is if we bring in the troops, half the world's gonna know something big is going on."

"And if our friends in the theater have notified everybody, like they said, the whole world knows anyway."

Tony nodded. "I guess you're right. Then I guess the question becomes, do we evacuate the area?"

"I don't think we can," the Chief said. "I think that was probably their point. By now, they've notified the press, radio, and TV. The phones are gonna start ringing any second. My guess is that the only thing we'll be able to do is keep people out, and that's probably going to cause problems. We'll need all the manpower we can get."

"Call Becker," Tony said. "Get the SWAT teams ready. Tell him we want every movable piece of equipment ready to roll. Everything. And get Stan to haul the off-duty boys in on the double. I'll get my own team ready. Other than that," Tony said, "I think the best we can do for now is set up a command post."

The Chief nodded, glancing at his watch. "I know the people who own that deli across from the theater. Call and see if we can use the place. This might be a long night. Anything else you can think of, Tony?"

Tony bit down on his cigar, eyes narrowing. "Probably a million things. But at this point, I don't think they really matter." He held the cigar between two fingers, pointing it in the general direction of the Chief. "I can't see giving in to their demands. I know your feelings, but I just can't see it. It's like giving every scumbag with the balls to try it a green light. I don't like it."

The Chief stood up suddenly. "We can't jeopardize 500 lives, Tony. We just can't take that risk, and that's final!"

Tony's jaw tightened, and he leaned back in his chair. "I don't think the final decision is going to be ours any longer."

"What's that supposed to mean?" the Chief demanded, his voice sharp.

"Exactly what I said. You may pull some strings in this town, Chief, but you're still one of the puppets."

The Chief's expression hardened, his fists clenched. "Enough, Tony," he warned. "Let's get down to the theater."

Before they could make it out the door, there was a knock.

"Excuse me, Sir," the sergeant said. "Ed Nelson from the Times."

The Chief nodded curtly. "You go ahead, Tony. I'll get you on the air as soon as I can get out of here."

Tony's thoughts drifted, his mind flickering back to his younger days.

He had always been a penny-ante gambler. The couple of times he'd been to Vegas had bugged him; he hated putting more than a couple of bucks into the slots, losing more than ten dollars at the blackjack table, or playing in anything but the smallest-time poker games. Tony worked too hard for his money. He didn't like to piss it away. That's the way Tony had been.

A few years ago, they'd paired Tony with a partner who played fast and loose. You name it, he'd bet it. Things changed. His partner finally talked him into going to the track.

Then the following week, they went again. And again. And again.

The first couple of times, they'd won. Won big. Tony had wheeled a Daryl MacHargue longshot, with almost everything running in the second race. His ingenuity was two-fold: Tony liked MacHargue as a jockey, and the horse's name was Nasty Nancy.

MacHargue's mount paid $8.80 to win. And, coupled with a heavy favorite ridden by Hawley in the second half of the double, the two-dollar daily was worth $108.60.

Soon, Tony was taking a serious interest in playing the horses. Before long, he was trying his own handicapping. He liked making mind bets almost as much as going to the track. On nights that he couldn't sleep, Tony would stop off at a liquor store and buy the racing form. He'd spend hours handicapping. More often than not, he'd just jot down his bets on paper. The next day, he'd check the results. It took only a short time before Tony became a handicapper and started to compare the results

Tony was running up a pretty good score, but most of it was on paper. When they switched him to days, he had to give up the track, except for his off days. So, like most people who play the ponies and can't get to the track, Tony did what came naturally: he got a book.

Being a cop, Tony had no trouble making contact. And being a cop, Tony had no trouble establishing credit.

Bookies are probably the most honest people alive. They have to be. Their business depends on their reputation.

At the beginning, Tony's action was light. A fin here, maybe a ten-spot there. But that was about it. On rare occasions, if something had looked really hot or someone had come up with a tip, Tony might have gone as high as twenty. But that had been Tony's limit.

He was ahead some $1,200 by the end of the third month.

Tony knew the risk he was taking. Hell, off-track betting was illegal. But that made it even more challenging and stimulating. Besides, who the hell was he really hurting? Tony enjoyed the luxuries that the added income afforded—his new clothes, some jewelry for Nancy, and a weekend here or there. Things that most cops couldn't afford. This was Tony's rationalization.

His first hundred-dollar bet was across the board. Gallant Lady, with MacHargue up, won by a length and a half. The winner paid $5.60, $4.00, and $3.40. Tony cursed himself for not betting the whole hundred on the nose. The next bet was straight up. The horse ran third.

Tony was still way ahead, and the loss didn't really bother him. But he doubled up on the next bet. Bet a little more the next time, and more the time after that. Before Tony realized it, he was in over his head. Now he was fighting to get out.

The book wasn't yet putting the squeeze on Tony. But what Tony was paying out of each paycheck was getting harder and harder to handle. A couple of horses, damn it! And he'd be out.

Yesterday, Tony had bet big on a horse called "Pocket Money." The horse ran out of money. Today, he was betting heavily on "Neat Claim." Hawley was up. The horse figured to cross the wire going away.

Tony held his breath as he pawed through the pages of the paper, looking for the late entries. If "Neat Claim" won, he wouldn't be out of the hole completely, but he'd be damn close. Then, it would be only a matter of another winner, and he'd be ahead again. Tony found the third race. He groaned. It was a sigh of relief. "Neat Claim" won. The horse paid $8.40.

Tony did some quick calculations. He had halved his tab. Tony swore that if he could only break even, if he could just wipe out that other 50%, he'd never touch another horse. Tony folded up the sheet and tossed it on the back seat.

He started the car, heading for the Mountain Theater. Tony was at Topanga Canyon and Victory Blvd in three minutes. The theater was on the southeast corner. He drove into the parking lot, cut the engine, and turned off the lights. Tony sat and watched. He wasn't sure what he was watching for or waiting for, but he wanted to get a feel for what was happening. He wanted to get his mind off the horses, off his financial situation, and on the present situation.

Tony stared at the marquee. The bright red letters boasted the title of the Halloween show.

Tony closed his eyes, trying to imagine what was going through the minds of the people inside that theater. The tension. The fear. The stark terror. Tony had seen some hard-core crap, but this was beyond reason.

Tony made mental notes as he looked around. The roof of the theater was flat. This meant there was plenty of cover for marksmen. There'd be no trouble situating the SWAT team on the roof. But Tony knew it wasn't going to do a hell of a lot of good.

Across the street was the huge shopping center's empty parking lot. There was plenty of open space. But would it be empty for long? They could bring in the units and headquarters them in the parking lot. Tony knew they'd have to move fast before the lookie-loos' lens came out.

Diagonally across the street, on the northwest corner, was a Mobil station, open 24 hours a day. Beyond that station was the residential area.

Across from the Mobil station was a Bank of America, a delicatessen, a drugstore, and a medical building. All closed for the night. The deli, the one the Chief wanted to use as a command post, had closed at 8:00. Across the street from the deli, south of the theater, was a small amusement park. Judging by the number of cars in the lot, Tony guessed the place was packed. That would create additional problems.

East of the theater sat a restaurant and a couple of bars. Tony knew the bars did a hell of a weekend business. This made the situation even more complex.

The first rule of police work is: wherever possible, protect innocent lives. Always avoid risks where risks can be avoided.

Tony could see no logical way out. They'd have to meet the demands. There was no answer. No safe solution. Tony shivered at what came into his mind: two million dollars, CASH. He shook his head as he started the engine.

Tony drove around the theater lot slowly. He made mental notes of all exit doors, all possible points of entry, and all possible points of escape.

The longer he drove, the more Tony realized they had their hands full. They couldn't storm the theater without risking hundreds of lives. After everything was said and done, there'd be only two options:

One pays the two million and hopes for a safe release of the hostages.

Refuse their demands and let them make the next move.

Tony completed his swing around the theater. He braked to stop in front of the marquee and leaned his head against the backrest, closing his eyes.

If this were Tony's ship, he knew exactly how he'd handle it. And that was probably exactly why it wasn't. From the very enactment of the stop-and-frisk law and the no-knock law some years ago, Tony was sure that Rome was doomed to fall.

The public thought the problem was within the department. They claimed there was a new breed of cop. It wasn't true. The problem was the inadequate laws. The antiquated criminal codes. The soft judicial system. When a cop is deprived of the right to stop and search, you can't enforce laws. Catch a suspect cold, and some smart-ass attorney makes you look like a fool because you didn't read the creep his rights properly.

More often than not, you'd have to get up on the stand and lie your fool head off to justify an arrest. When you came right down to it, it had little to do with the cop. It was the laws. And when you came right down to it, the decent citizen was getting screwed. Laws that were designed to protect the citizens were actually doing the opposite. They were protecting the criminal.

If Tony had his way, certain crimes would automatically assure the death penalty: kidnapping, rape, murder, pushing hard-core drugs, and selling handguns to kids. These crimes should carry a mandatory death penalty. Let the sociologists argue themselves blue about its ineffectiveness. Tony knew darn well the death penalty was a necessary evil. One of the easiest crimes to get away with today is murder. The criminal has the law working for him.

Today, the law shows more concern for the criminal than for the victim. This wasn't the first time, Tony realized, that a stunt like this had been tried. When the first plane was hijacked, if the authorities had done what Tony would have done, there would have been a swift end to plane hijackings.

Tony would have taken the first set of hijackers, put them against a wall, and machine-gunned them in the town square.

Tony considered certain crimes to be atrocities. They should carry special penalties. No trial. No waste of time or taxpayers' money. Kill them and get it over with.

Anybody who'd pull a stunt like that was a major threat to society. A threat to society didn't deserve to live.

But Tony was part of the legal system and not a politician. Tony had to abide, not fight it. At least, not the way he wanted to fight it.

Tony searched in his pocket for a cigar; at the same time, he reached for the radio. The Chief told Tony what Tony had already concluded. The TV and radio people had gotten hold of the mass kidnapping. It was now public knowledge. Tony looked at his watch. He wondered how long he had until the thrill-seekers hit the pavement.

They were bound to have curious onlookers on the spot. It would mean valuable manpower wasted on crowd control. It would mean a loss of investigative manpower. In short, it would mean additional risk to innocent victims. Tony bit off the end of his cigar and spat it out the window.

3:00 P.M.

DANNY'S DILEMMA (THE ADDICT)

Some people rely on a power greater than themselves—a husband, a wife, a child, God. Danny Knight's higher power was drugs and heroin. But Danny's god betrayed him. His god's services were expensive, and Danny was out of money.

He searched his mind for anyone he hadn't put the bite on, but Danny had run out of names. And the pain was rapidly growing unbearable.

Brandy's Liquor Store was on the north side of Sherman Way, a block east of Canoga Avenue. It had been a family-run operation for 50 years, dating back to when Canoga Park was an upper-middle-class neighborhood. But over time, it had given way to so-called packaged apartments and lower-class housing. The area was now home to small businesses, working-class Mexicans, and the hard-core unemployed. The police spent hundreds of man-hours patrolling the areas bordering the poorer sections of Canoga Park, dedicating just as much effort to containing crime there.

Brandy's was one of only three liquor stores within a ten-mile radius that remained open until the state-regulated 2 a.m. closing time. The majority of liquor stores shut their doors at 9 p.m., especially on Sunday nights. Some stretched their hours to midnight, but Brandy's was after the extra buck—hence the 2 a.m. closing.

Before Danny Knight became addicted, he had often tripped

out on grass and wine. He could get the grass anywhere, but he almost always got the wine at Brandy's. He had been in the store often and knew the layout almost better than the people who worked there.

He was puzzled by the high turnover among the liquor store clerks. It seemed that whenever he went in, there was a new face behind the counter. It surprised him because clerking in a liquor store didn't seem that difficult. As a matter of fact, Danny had seriously considered asking the owner for a job.

But now, completely strung out and trying to blink back the sun, the words "Brandy's Liquor" kept flashing in Danny's mind. He tried to push them away. He couldn't. As the knot in his gut tightened, he realized why that sign kept reappearing in his thoughts.

Danny was standing not more than a hundred feet from the liquor store, staring—not at the sun, but directly into the red flashing neon sign: "BRANDY'S LIQUOR STORE."

Danny laughed. But it wasn't funny.

He was about to enter a world known by few, survived by even fewer—a world completely his own.

Danny was past that thin line—he'd crossed it some time ago. Now, he had only two choices: withdraw cold turkey or continue down his road. A road that led to a dead end.

But Danny wasn't quite ready to go cold turkey. Not yet. He had to have his fix... just one more time.

He looked at his watch. He was good for maybe another hour,

an hour and a half tops, before the pain would become completely unbearable. Excruciating. By that time, he'd be damned near delirious—and then he would be delirious. It would be too late... he'd be picked up. Picked up in an alley... on the street... picked up. And once the cops got him, there wouldn't be any treatment. Just a cell until he was processed. And Danny couldn't take that. Not now. He'd been there too many times. He wasn't going there again.

Danny groped again for the name of someone he could turn to. There had to be somebody he could put the bite on for a few bucks. But his list of names had dwindled to none. Most of his remaining acquaintances were tapped out, dead, or in jail. The few who were left didn't give a shit about Danny.

He turned and started walking back to his home—the backseat of a 1968 Dodge. The floor of the car held a change of jeans, a pair of socks, and some boots. And then, suddenly, a picture flashed in his mind.

Under the seat of that car was a .38.

Danny quickly looked back at the flashing neon sign of Brandy's. His mind framed the .38 under the seat. He squeezed his eyes shut, trying to erase the image, but his mind had locked onto it, just like it had locked onto that sign.

There had to be another way out.

All the way back to the Dodge, Danny kept telling himself that. But he couldn't think of one. There wasn't a single name he could come up with. No one who might be willing to help.

No one could con, scam, or sweet-talk him into giving him some money. No one he hadn't already burned.

No one.

Danny might have been a lot of things. But one thing he wasn't—not yet—was a thief.

6:00 P.M.

BARBARA'S GOODBYE (JULIE'S MOM)

Barbara watched from the living room window as Gene backed the Continental out of the driveway. She waved to her husband as the taillights dimmed in the distance. As Barbara watched the Continental disappear, she thought about their daughter, Julie.

Just yesterday, she had been their little girl—a baby still in diapers. Now, Julie was thirteen. Almost a young lady. Ready for her first date. Barbara blinked back tears, turned away from the window, and walked into the kitchen. She glanced at the wall clock over the sink.

"Hurry up, honey!" she yelled up the stairs. "You don't want to be late." Then, as an afterthought, she added, "Can I help?"

"No," Julie's determined voice replied. "I'm almost ready, Mommy. I'll be down in half a minute."

Barbara sat down at the kitchen table and stared into her coffee cup, trying to relax. But she knew her reaction was normal. Most mothers would feel the same way.

She thought back to her own first date. And even though times were different, some things never changed. What trouble—she asked herself—could Julie possibly get into at a movie theater? Especially one as well-supervised as... she searched for the right word... as classy as the Mountain

Theater.

Particularly on a night when they were having a special Halloween show.

What possible trouble could her daughter get into?

It wasn't as if she were going out with some boy nobody knew. Bryan Winkler—three years older than her daughter—was an honor student, the son of one of their best friends, and a clerk at the local Food King after school.

Barbara lit a cigarette and glanced at the clock. She was about to call out to Julie when she heard her on the stairs.

She turned and watched, choking back tears, as the thirteen-year-old—more woman now than a child—walked into the kitchen.

Barbara may have been biased, but to her, Julie was stunning. She was radiant in her long, flowing red gown. The cut of the dress made her breasts appear fuller. It was the dress Julie had insisted on when they went shopping.

Julie looked up at the clock. "See?" she said, trying to hide her own nervousness. "I've even got time for a Coke."

Barbara smiled and nodded. She got up and walked around the table to her daughter. Then she buried her face in Julie's shoulder. Julie could feel her mother's tears running down her arm. She felt her own tears welling up in her eyes.

6:30 P.M.

GUN AND A PLAN (DANNY)

Danny's hand searched under the seat of the Dodge until his fingers touched something cold and foreign. He stared at it for several seconds, then opened the chamber to make sure it was loaded.

He buried the .38 in the waistband of his pants, under his shirt, and got out of the car, carefully locking the door behind him. Frantically, he tried to force his brain to come up with a name. Someone, anyone, he could turn to.

It was useless.

Before Danny even realized it, he was already halfway down the street leading to Brandy's. At least, he thought, his timing was right. It was 6:30, already dark. Most people would be at home having dinner or getting ready to go out. The liquor store wouldn't be crowded.

He hoped there wouldn't be anyone inside.

Danny didn't want to do this. But time was running out. It would probably take him at least half an hour to find his connection after he got the money. And if there were customers in the store, he'd have to wait.

Shit!

He was nervous. Danny reassured himself by patting the cold steel of the gun in his waistband. He quickened his pace. The knot in his stomach tightened. The nausea grew more intense.

Was it nerves or withdrawal?

He wasn't in enough control to figure it out. Probably a combination of the two.

He'd been down this road before.

Danny knew the feelings. He knew what came next. He knew exactly how much pain he could take before he started to lose his mind. And he knew he couldn't take much more.

Not this time. Not again.

This time, Danny promised himself it would be absolutely the last.

He'd get help after this. If he had to, he'd go to the hospital. He'd beat this thing. Straighten out. Shape up. They'd see. He'd show them all.

All the people who had told him he'd end up strung out in the streets.

He'd prove them wrong.

This fix, Danny swore to his god, would be the last fix. This was going to be the end.

Danny stopped in front of the liquor store window. He peered inside. A young, moustachioed Mexican stood at the counter. A pregnant woman stood beside him. Danny looked toward the back of the store.

Nobody.

He turned—and saw a black-and-white police cruiser

approaching.

Just cruising, Danny whispered to himself. Relax. He's just cruising.

He kept his eyes on the car until it passed.

When the Mexican and the woman left the store, Danny walked in.

He didn't head straight to the counter. Instead, he went to the back of the store. He killed a couple of minutes thumbing through the girlie magazines, then moved toward the freezer section, where they kept the cold sodas and beer.

He wanted to be sure there was no one else inside.

Danny didn't see anybody.

His fingers brushed against the gun in his waistband.

Then he walked toward the counter.

He was ten feet away when the door opened.

Two customers walked in.

Danny snapped his fingers and cursed under his breath.

"Forgot the beer," he muttered, turning around. He hurried back to the coolers, breathing a sigh of relief as he reached the beer.

He didn't want to do this.

He really wasn't up to it.

If there was any other way out at all, he'd gladly take it.

But Danny couldn't hack the agony of withdrawal. Not again. Not now. Not yet.

He had to prepare himself mentally. He had to get psyched.

It wasn't fair.

If he'd only known, he never would have started on this long journey to hell. If he'd only known where it would lead, he never would have taken that first hit. But like most kids who get hooked, Danny thought he was different.

It wouldn't be like what he'd heard.

In his case, Danny knew it was going to be different.

He laughed bitterly.

All his life, Danny had been telling himself this time would be different.

Maybe now, it would finally be.

Danny watched as the two guys at the counter paid for their cigarettes and left. He glanced around quickly. No one else is in the store. No more reason to stall.

He had to get it over with.

Ten feet from the counter, Danny pressed the gun into his hand.

The clerk's back was turned.

Danny coughed.

The clerk turned around. He was thick-shouldered, heavyset. One gold tooth glinted in the front of his mouth, looking almost comical. He was fifty, but Danny figured they were fifty street years. The man looked hard.

Danny clutched his gut with his left hand. With his right hand, he pushed the gun forward. His legs felt unsteady.

The clerk's eyes flicked from the gun to Danny's face. Then back to the gun. Then back to Danny.

Danny knew he was being sized up.

He shook his head defiantly.

"No," Danny said. "Don't get cute. No tricks. Just give me the money, and you won't get hurt."

The Mexican hesitated.

"I'm not fucking with you, man," Danny snapped. "I mean business. If I don't get what I need, I'm going to die anyway. Get the picture?"

He flicked a glance at the window. Nobody outside. Not even a car on the street.

"It's not your money," Danny said, half-pleading. "Open the register!"

The clerk nodded.

Danny felt a slight wave of relief wash over him. But his grip on the gun was slick with sweat. His fingers were stiffening around the trigger.

He watched carefully as the Mexican opened the register. He needed to be sure the man didn't push any hidden buttons.

Danny's confidence grew as the clerk pulled the bills from the register and stuffed them into a paper sack.

"Under the tray," Danny reminded him. He knew they always kept the bigger bills underneath.

The clerk shot him a resentful glance but obeyed, lifting the tray and pulling out a few more bills. He shoved them into the sack and slid it across the counter.

Danny grabbed a Playboy magazine from the rack and laid it on top of the bag. He wrapped the paper tightly around it, disguising the money.

Then he motioned for the greasy-haired clerk to step out from behind the counter.

"In the back," Danny ordered. "Move!"

He walked the clerk into the storeroom.

"Lie down. On your stomach."

The man turned, staring at Danny. Their eyes locked.

"Don't worry," Danny said. "I'm not going to hurt you. I got what I wanted. Now I just need time to get away."

The Mexicans believed him. He lay flat on his stomach on the cold, dirty floor.

Danny knelt over him and struck him once behind the ear with the butt of the gun.

Quickly, he ran out of the storeroom, out of the liquor store.

Onto Sherman Way.

He started walking back to his car.

His home.

8:00 P.M.

INTO THE THEATRE (JULIE & BRYAN)

Tears welled in Barbara's eyes as she watched her daughter, Julie, and Julie's date, Bryan, walk hand in hand into the lobby of the Mountain Theater.

Her baby was growing up.

Someday, Julie would be married, with children of her own. The thought tightened Barbara's chest. She wiped her eyes quickly, put the station wagon in gear, and drove out of the parking lot onto Topanga Canyon Blvd.

Julie and Bryan held hands, their palms damp with nervous sweat, as they stood in front of the refreshment stand, waiting for their buttered popcorn. The scent of melted butter and fresh-popped kernels filled the air.

To ease the awkward silence between them, they watched the people filing into the lobby in costume. The distraction helped.

When their popcorn finally arrived, Bryan paid and held out the bag to Julie.

She took a handful, nodding her thanks.

"Let's stand over there." She pointed to an out-of-the-way corner. "We'll be able to see better."

Bryan nodded quickly. Anything was better than standing here, fumbling for words. It wasn't that he didn't like Julie—

he just didn't know what to say.

Julie watched as two men entered, one dressed as the Lone Ranger, the other as Tonto. The sight triggered childhood memories.

"Too bad we didn't wear costumes," she mused.

"No," Bryan blurted out. "That would've been dumb. That's kid stuff."

The second the words left his mouth, he regretted them.

Adults in costume were all around them.

"Well…" He grabbed more popcorn. "Maybe next Halloween."

Julie let it slide, her attention shifting to a group walking through the entrance—a woman dressed as Snow White, followed by seven kids, each one in a different dwarf costume. She laughed. The idea was terrific. If she were judging the contest, she'd definitely give them a prize.

"How about something to drink?" Bryan asked, breaking her concentration.

Julie nodded. The salty popcorn had made her thirsty.

"Hold this," he said, handing her the bag. "I'll be right back."

As she waited, Julie kept watching the crowd. Some costumes were simple, just masks, while others were elaborate. Some were clearly store-bought, others homemade.

She admired the Lone Ranger and Tonto again. Even if their

costumes weren't unique, they still reminded her of childhood. She could almost hear the cry— "Hi-Yo Silver! Away!"

Bryan's voice pulled her back.

"Here." He handed her a Coke. "Better hurry. The show's gonna start soon."

Julie glanced at the lobby. Only a few people were still buying tickets.

She took a long sip of soda. The cold fizz washed down her throat, instantly refreshing. When she looked back at Bryan, she smiled.

She realized, despite being three years older, he was at least as nervous as she was.

And suddenly, she felt in control.

"Where do you like to sit?"

Bryan shrugged. "Anywhere you want."

Julie thought for a moment.

"Let's sit in the middle."

"Okay," he said quickly, crunching a piece of ice.

Julie reached for his hand, squeezing it reassuringly.

Hand in hand, they walked inside to find their seats.

6:55 P.M.

PREPPING FOR THE SCORE (THE HEIST CREW)

Danny felt a rush of relief as he walked back toward the Dodge. Another half hour, and he'd have his fix.

The robbery hadn't been as bad as he'd expected. Nerve-wrecking? Sure. But that was natural.

He hadn't liked hitting the guy.

But he had to. If he hadn't, the clerk would've been on the phone with the cops the second Danny walked out the door.

Danny opened the Dodge's door, slid into the backseat, and pulled it shut. He checked the street—empty. Satisfied, he reached into his waistband, slid the gun out carefully, and shoved it under the seat.

Next, he pulled the paper bag from his shirt and dumped the money onto the seat. He didn't even bother counting it. He stuffed the bills into his pocket and let out a long sigh.

The knot in his stomach clenched tighter. He rubbed his gut and climbed out of the car, heading west. Just a few more minutes. Just a few more minutes.

He kept repeating it like a prayer.

At Jordan Street, he turned right. The cockroach-infested apartments loomed on the corner of Jordan and Haskell. They should've been condemned years ago, but instead, they were rented out for a minimum of $150 a month.

Danny rapped on the door. Hard.

"What do you want?" a voice asked.

"It's me. Danny. Open the door."

"Danny, who? I don't know any Danny."

Danny's mind was foggy. He'd forgotten the code words.

His pulse pounded. He knew those words like his own name.

"Little Tiger," he rasped. "Little Tiger. Now open the fuckin' door."

The door creaked open, just wide enough for Danny to slip inside.

The room reeked of mildew and cigarette smoke. A rickety wooden cocktail table and two wobbly chairs sat in the center. Paint chips flaked from the walls, cracks split the ceiling, and cobwebs thickened every corner.

Danny swallowed hard. He felt like he'd just stepped into the Vegas Hilton.

To his right stood Joey.

At five-ten, Joey was two inches taller than Danny, with a round belly and a polished appearance. His hair was combed to perfection, his skin smooth, his blue eyes cold.

Danny clutched his stomach.

"I'm hurtin'," he rasped. "Bad. I need some shit. I need it now."

Joey wagged his head from side to side.

"You got bread?"

Danny nodded, fingers twitching as he pulled out a wad of bills.

Joey looked surprised. "Figured we'd seen the last of you."

Danny shifted from foot to foot, his nerves spiking. The pain was climbing fast now, tearing through his gut.

Joey was stalling. Playing games. Probably angling for more money.

Danny wasn't having it.

He doubled over, pressing a fist to his stomach, wishing he had the gun.

He liked the feel of the cold steel in his palm.

Danny locked eyes with Joey. His voice was low, sharp.

"Don't fuck with me, Joey."

Joey shrugged. "I got to get it, Danny. We were just closing down for the afternoon." He glanced at his watch, rubbing his chin thoughtfully. "Meet me in the men's room at the Mountain Theater. Eight o'clock sharp."

Panic shot through Danny.

"I can't wait that long," he gasped. "I can't."

Joey studied him for a moment. Then, with a sigh, he said, "I'll give you a little something to hold you over. The rest at eight."

Relief flooded Danny. He nodded gratefully.

At least he'd get temporary relief.

But this was it.

This was the last time.

He tipped his head back, staring at the crack in the ceiling, and swore—to whoever was up there—he would never put the needle in his arm again.

4:45 P.M.

THE PEARSONS PREPARE (COSTUME CHAOS)

The Pearsons were a well-liked young family in the upper-middle-class neighbourhood of Woodland Hills. Don, his pretty wife June, and their four daughters lived in a two-story house just south of the Boulevard, right across from the elementary school the girls attended.

Don taught eighth-grade English at a local junior high. June was a fifth-grade math teacher.

As Don pulled into the driveway, he switched off the radio, put the car in park, and set the emergency brake. He was smiling as he stepped out of the car. He had every reason to smile—he was young, happy, and had a beautiful family. And it was Halloween.

He held the screen door so it wouldn't slam and made a mental note—again—to fix the damn thing.

"I'm home, honey."

"I'm upstairs! Be right down."

Don tossed his sports jacket over his favorite living room chair and wandered into the kitchen. As usual, June had left The Times open on the table. He got lost in the sports section and didn't even hear her come in.

"Hi, hon." She kissed his cheek lightly. "Good day?"

Don kept his eyes on the paper. "Quiet. You?"

"Fine."

"Where are the kids?"

June sat down. "Softball practice, the library, piano lessons, and Ellie's house—putting the finishing touches on a Halloween costume."

Don folded the newspaper and set it aside. They're going to a party?"

June hesitated. "Sort of."

Don reached for the corner of the newspaper, toying with its edge. "What's that supposed to mean?"

"Well…" She was stalling. "I kind of promised the girls they could go to a Halloween costume party."

Don shrugged. "So? Sounds fine to me."

"I also told Ed and Jean that Ellie could go along."

"That's fine." He said it, but his gut told him there was more.

"Well…"

Don smiled. "Spit it out."

"The party is at the Mountain Theater. It's a double feature. Two spooky movies, a costume contest…"

Don sighed. "I think I get the idea…"

"Not quite." June hesitated. "I didn't want the kids to go alone. I thought they needed a chaperone…"

Don pointed between them. "Chaperones?"

"Chaperones," June confirmed. "But honey, it'll be fun. You'll see. Especially in your costume."

Don sat up straighter. "What costume?"

"We designed them, honey. That's what Linda's doing at Ellie's house. Finishing hers."

"You mean we're wearing costumes?"

"Well, of course! What kind of Halloween party would it be if we didn't?"

Don was no longer smiling. Not because he was mad—he actually found the whole thing hilarious—but he wasn't about to let June know that.

"I'm almost afraid to ask. Nope. I take that back. I am afraid. What are the costumes?"

"Would you believe…" June grinned. "Snow White and the Seven Dwarfs?"

"Snow White and the…" Don groaned. "You gotta be kidding."

"Wait till you see them!" June cut in, rushing past his protest. "The kids did a fantastic job."

"I'm sure," Don said dryly. "Any other surprises?"

June glanced at the kitchen clock. "We've got almost an hour before the kids are home." Her voice turned mischievous. "Let's go upstairs. I'll show you my costume."

Don smirked. "Trick or treat?"

7:25 P.M.

Waiting on a Fix (Danny)

Danny Knight paced the theater lobby nervously, trying to drink a Coke. The effort was wasted. He was spilling more on his shirt than he was getting in his mouth. His hands were shaking, his mouth was dry, and his nose was running. Danny Knight was in bad shape—very bad shape.

He looked at his watch. 7:28.

"Son of a bitch," he muttered. "Where the fuck is he?"

Danny didn't know how much more of this he could take. He was getting scared. Panicky.

His stomach was on fire. His knees were weak. With an all-out effort, he managed to walk over to the trash can and toss the Coke away. He thought about heading to the restroom to wash his face, but he wasn't sure he'd make it. His legs felt like rubber.

Danny was afraid.

He was about to collapse.

Somehow, someway, somewhere—there had to be a better way.

Danny watched as people entered the theater. His vision blurred. He was sure he was hallucinating.

It had finally happened. He had lost his mind.

People who were dead were walking into the theatre.

Danny blinked hard, trying to clear the images, but they refused to disappear. Napoleon walked in. A few feet behind him, Moses strolled through the doors, carrying the Ten Commandments.

Danny rubbed his eyes.

And then he started laughing.

A hysterical, breathless laughter.

He opened his eyes.

In walked Snow White, followed by the Seven Dwarfs.

And then the Lone Ranger.

Danny shook his head. No fucking way. There he was, the Lone Ranger, with Tonto at his side.

He turned and forced himself toward the men's room. Sweat poured down his face. The short walk was agony.

Danny tried to think of anything else—anything—but it was useless.

He fought back the nausea he knew could only end in dry heaves. He had nothing left in his stomach to puke up.

Danny wished he had the gun. If only he'd brought it. Maybe he'd finally do what he should have done a long time ago.

Then he wouldn't have to worry about his next fix.

About kicking the habit.

About jail.

About cold turkey.

About a fix.

About withdrawing.

About another fix.

About cold turkey.

About another fix…

Danny didn't remember getting there.

But his hands were cupped under the tap, splashing cold water on his face. It didn't kill the pain deep in his gut, but it washed away the nausea.

His legs felt stronger. He crossed the tile floor to the towel dispenser.

Danny looked at his watch. 7:40.

Cocksucker.

He'd kill the prick.

That asshole was a sadistic motherfucker. He was doing this on purpose.

He loved torturing Danny.

He knew what happened when Danny didn't get his fix. He knew how close he was to going over the line.

"Christ," Danny thought. "Just one last chance. Just let me

make it this one time. I'll show you. I know you don't believe me, but give me this one last chance!"

Danny turned suddenly.

He'd been alone in the restroom. But now—now he was sure he heard footsteps.

Then he saw the face in the mirror.

"Relax, Danny Boy. It's me—your Messiah."

If he didn't have what Danny needed, Danny swore he was going to kill him.

He'd tear him apart with his bare hands.

"First, the money," Messiah said, holding out his hand.

Danny forced his trembling fingers into his pockets. He pulled out wads of bills—and kept dropping them.

Messiah stared down at the cash. "What'd you do, rob the B of A?"

Fuck you, Danny thought. You little cocksucker.

"I sold my car."

Messiah laughed. But when the restroom door creaked open, he bent down quickly, scooping up the fallen bills.

Once the third party finished his business and left, Messiah and Danny completed their deal.

As Messiah walked out, Danny stepped into a stall, shut the door, locked it, took off his jacket, rolled up his sleeve—

And put the needle in his arm.

Twenty minutes later, as the lights of the Mountain Theater dimmed, Danny Knight leaned back in his seat.

That high—that rush—

There was no feeling like it in the world.

4:00 P.M.

FORBIDDEN LOVE (MAC & NANCY)

Mac forced his head back against the pillow, his eyes tightly closed. He kicked at the covers, and they fell to the floor.

"You're beautiful, baby," he whispered. "You're absolutely fantastic."

And it was beautiful—more beautiful than anything he had ever known before. Mac reached down and stroked her long, soft blonde hair. He only wished it would never end. He only wished she could keep on licking the head of his cock forever.

Mac felt himself growing harder, longer, as Nancy's lips alternately sucked and stroked.

Nancy was what every woman should be—a lady outside the bedroom, a whore in the bedroom. What a way to live! Mac thought, reaching under her to finger her nipple.

"You're driving me insane," Mac whispered. Deep down inside, he felt like a king—he was somewhere he'd never been before.

Nancy was making soft, guttural sounds—groaning noises—as her tongue worked on Mac's shaft. Her free hand found his crotch, and Nancy toyed with his anus. Just when Mac had decided that nothing could send him to greater peaks, Nancy found a way.

Mac took long, deep breaths, trying to fight the sensation he knew was bringing him to the point of no return. He wasn't ready yet. His fingernails clawed at the sheets. He reached behind him, grabbing the headboard. Mac heard Nancy groan more urgently. He felt himself growing harder, throbbing.

Quickly, suddenly, Mac reached for her legs and pulled them over his shoulders. He buried his face between her legs and tasted her sweetness. Now, he heard her groaning softly. Her pace slackened. Mac focused his attention on pleasing her. He tasted her juices. His tongue found its way inside her, bringing her closer to ecstasy. The deeper his tongue explored, the more frenzied she became. And for one moment, Mac thought she was going to devour him.

Nancy tongued his testicles. She took the shaft of his penis in her mouth. She deep-throated him, taking in more and more of his penis.

Just when he was certain neither of them could take any more, Nancy suddenly stopped. Mac knew what she wanted, and he gave it to her.

Nancy clawed at his back with her long fingernails as she reached her climax. Her excitement was bringing on his own climax. He felt her shuddering—not once, not twice, but three times. With each urgent shudder of her own, his thrusts became deeper and deeper and deeper until he exploded within her.

Finally, they collapsed in each other's arms, holding one another contentedly before they fell asleep, clutched in embrace.

Nancy awoke first. She shook him gently.

When he awoke, he was momentarily startled—then he got his bearings.

"What time is it?"

"Five-thirty."

"I guess we dozed."

"Only about half an hour," she said.

Mac straddled her as he reached for his cigarettes.

As his hand touched the cigarette pack on the night table, Nancy pushed his hand away. Mac fell on top of her. He looked into Nancy's soft blue eyes, and Mac knew what Nancy wanted.

But suddenly, Mac felt uncomfortable. And he knew why. He closed his eyes and clenched his fist around the cigarette pack.

Nancy remained still. Mac lit two cigarettes, passing one to Nancy. He lay back against the pillow and inhaled deeply, thoughtfully.

Nancy lay her head on Mac's shoulder.

"What did I do?"

Mac blew the smoke away from her. He shook his head.

"Nothing, angel. It's not you. Nothing."

"Then, what is it?"

"Us. The situation. My feelings. This house. The fact that

your husband's a cop. Do you have any idea what it's like making love to someone you love, knowing that buried in the back of my mind is the fear that at any time, that door could open and I could end up with a .38 up my ass?"

Mac took a long, deep drag of his cigarette.

Nancy's frown turned to a grin, and her gaze went from the bottom of Mac's feet to the top of his head.

"It's not a .38," she said, staring squarely into Mac's eyes. "Tony carries a .357 Magnum."

Mac laughed, but his heart wasn't in it.

"Very funny!"

"I'm sorry, honey," Nancy said, sincerely meaning it. "I guess it's time we came to a decision."

And then she rolled over.

8:00 A.M.

ROOKIE ON PATROL (OFFICER HUFFINGTON)

October 31—Halloween—was a special day for John Huffington. It marked an anniversary: his sixteenth month as a West Valley policeman.

John was 24 years old and single. He liked his job and loved life. He was working the 8 a.m. to 4 p.m. swing shift. And because of the holiday, he was assigned an "L" car, meaning he was working without a partner.

Today wasn't the first day John had worked alone. He disliked not having a partner to talk with, but he liked the chance to be alone with his thoughts.

He reached across the seat to his right, found the small transistor radio, and switched it on. He began to hum along with the old Elvis tunes. John glanced at his watch. It was five past nine. He slowed for a light. As it changed, he eased the black-and-white into the right lane, then turned onto Roscoe.

John drove slowly, checking out several used car lots and watching the lot boys hose down cars. A couple more paychecks, and he'd have the down payment for a new car. His old Ford had just about had it.

At the next light, he turned right and headed south on Canoga. He passed a bowling alley and a drive-in theater. He was a quarter-mile north of Saticoy when he noticed a white Caddie convertible making a sharp right turn off Saticoy, heading south on Canoga at high speed.

John didn't accelerate. He followed leisurely, observing. The Caddie was gaining distance. He checked his speedometer—he was doing thirty-five. The Caddie was doing forty-five, maybe fifty.

John stepped down on the accelerator, increasing his speed to forty. The Caddie was still pulling away. He knew there was a dangerous S-curve up ahead. At its current speed, the Caddie was going to have trouble negotiating the turn.

John eyed the taillights. He didn't see the brake lights flash, but he heard tires squealing as the Caddie shot across the solid white line. He shook his head. It was a damned good thing there wasn't any oncoming traffic. He hit the lights and the siren and pushed the accelerator to the floor.

The driver of the Caddie seemed oblivious to the patrol car, the siren, and the flashing reds. For a split second, John expected a chase. But with the black-and-white now just a couple of feet from the Caddie's bumper, it pulled to the curb.

Ticket book in his left hand, John eased himself out of the car. His right hand hovered near the butt of his Magnum. He approached cautiously. He saw long blonde hair and figured he'd snagged a smart-ass hippie teenager.

John relaxed when he saw a pair of hands locked around the Caddie's steering wheel. Bending slightly, he lowered his head to the window and flipped open the ticket book.

The light-skinned, green-eyed woman looked about twenty-five. She smiled invitingly. In a deep Southern drawl, she asked, “What can I do for y’all?”

John glanced down at her bare legs and the fire-engine red miniskirt hiked up over her very shapely thighs. He wondered what was under the skirt. He must have seen better legs before, but he couldn’t remember where. He repeated his request, though he would have preferred to be requesting something else.

“Ma’am, your license and registration, please.”

She smiled and nodded, thumbing through her purse.

John hoped she’d have trouble finding it. He was suddenly in no hurry. He was enjoying the view immensely.

“Here ‘tis, honey,” she said sweetly, holding out a black wallet.

“Take out the license, please, ma’am.”

“Whatever did I do, officer?”

“You were pushing it, ma’am. Just a bit.”

“The speed limit is thirty-five, isn’t it? I’m sure I saw a sign...”

“Yes, ma’am,” John agreed, taking the license. “But you were exceeding the limit by at least ten miles an hour.”

“Oh, my, my,” she said. “It’s so hard to judge the speed in a big, heavy car.”

“Is the car registered to you, ma’am?”

"Heavens, no. It's my agent's. I can't afford anything like this anyway."

"Your agent, ma'am?"

Green Eyes nodded. "I'm an actress. Well, really, I'm hoping to be an actress. So far, I've only done one commercial. But my agent says I've got real talent."

"Yes, ma'am."

John sneaked another look at those legs. She sure did have talent—if she learned how to use it. She'd undoubtedly make it big.

He studied the license carefully. He knew why he was hesitating. Hell. The ticket was justified—she had it coming—but he really didn't want to write it. He'd much rather spend the rest of his shift staring at those thighs.

John looked into her green eyes. "Ma'am, excuse me a minute. I'm going to run a check on the car. If everything checks out, we'll let you off with a warning."

She blinked several times. "How can I ever thank you, Sergeant?"

John sighed. He didn't bother correcting her. Instead, he walked back to the squad car. The Caddie came back clean, registered with a North Hollywood talent agency. He dropped the mic on the seat and returned to the Caddie.

"Ma'am," he said, handing Green Eyes her license. "I hope you take this warning seriously. It really should be a citation."

She nodded. "I promise you, Sergeant. I'll watch all the signs."

"I'm sure," John said. As he walked away from the Caddie, he cursed himself for being a sucker for a pair of shapely thighs.

The rest of the morning was quiet and uneventful. At 12:30, John requested Code 7 for his lunch break but was told to answer a prowler call—Code 2. He turned the black-and-white around and sped north.

Before knocking on the door, he made sure his gun was in position at his side. The little old lady who greeted him was at least 182. Her face was wrinkled, and her steel-gray hair was neatly combed. As she spoke, John noticed how much effort it took her to form the words.

She opened the door just wide enough for John to squeeze inside. Despite his first impression, he realized she was a sweet old lady.

"What seems to be the trouble, ma'am?"

She pointed toward the window.

"Do you think somebody's out there?" John asked, unsnapping his holster.

She nodded.

If anything was out there, John figured it was just kids playing Halloween pranks. Nonetheless, his hand remained ready on the butt of his gun. He tiptoed the short distance to the window. Standing to one side, he pushed at the frame. The window slid open easily.

And then, it all happened in a nerve-shattering split second.

John yanked the pistol from its holster. As he drew the weapon, he hit the floor, flat. At that exact instant, he aimed and cocked the .357. He was coiled and ready.

It took a fraction longer for the events to register.

When they did, John reacted in two ways.

First, he squeezed his ass cheeks together because, otherwise, he was sure he'd shit his pants.

Second, he blinked his eyes tightly shut and holstered his gun.

He was too damned embarrassed to face the old lady.

The old gal stood over him. In a steady voice, she asked, "Are you all right, son?"

John tried to steady his shaking legs as he stood up. Once he regained some composure, he brushed himself off. At least, he thought, the floor was clean.

"Your cat?" he asked, walking toward the door.

The old lady nodded innocently.

John drove back to the station for Code 7.

The next few hours of patrol were routine. Between 1:30 and 3:30, he wrote three tickets—one to a teenager for speeding, one to a middle-aged woman for rolling through a stop sign, and one to a pimply-faced youngster for jaywalking.

John tried to bury the cat incident, but it wouldn't stay dead.

He wondered if the damn thing had nine lives. He just hoped to hell none of the other cops found out about it. If they did, he'd be the laughingstock of West Valley.

He glanced at his watch. His shift was almost over. He drove slowly, trying to kill the remaining minutes.

Half a block from the station, he saw it—the white Caddie convertible. The one he had let off with a warning earlier.

At first glance, it looked like the driver had just done a sloppy job of parking the big car. A closer inspection told the real story. The Caddie was wrapped around a tree.

John made a quick U-turn mid-block, flipped on the flashing reds, and pulled up. From the looks of the accident, the car had been heading north on DeSoto when the driver lost control and slammed into the tree. Judging by the damage, she had been really moving. The impact had crushed the passenger side, near the door.

John cursed himself for not writing her that ticket.

He spotted a tow truck driver nearby and called out.

The young man, wearing greasy coveralls, recognized him.

"What's up?" he asked. "The other officer already got the info."

John nodded. "Was the driver a young blonde?"

"Yeah," the tow truck driver said. "I watched them cut her out of the car. I got here right after the ambulance, so I saw most of it. She was lucky. Except for busted teeth, she didn't seem too badly broken up. She was coherent. I guess the steering wheel got her mouth. Hell, she even argued about going to the hospital. Kept saying that speed scared her."

John shook his head.

It was a damned shame that cops didn't scare her.

It was also a damned shame that he'd been more interested in legs than law enforcement.

He took one last look at the wrecked Caddie.

Without checking the time, he decided his shift was over. He walked back to the cruiser, got in, and headed for the station.

John figured he'd earned his pay for the day.

He also figured he needed a night out.

He made a mental note to call Gloria from the station. Take her to dinner. A show.

He needed peace and quiet.

And Gloria was usually good for the peace.

8:00 P.M.

SHOWTIME BEGINS (INSIDE THE THEATRE)

Gene hit the arrow and watched the ball roll toward the headpin. At the last second, the ball hooked and took down all ten pins. Gene grinned as he walked off the lane, picking up his beer as he sat down.

Gene glanced at the automatic scoring device overhead. According to the tally, his team was ahead by twenty-two pins going into the tenth and final frame. If they could get four out of five marks in the last frame, they'd have a lock on the game.

He took a long, cold swallow of beer, then turned to the fellow next to him, slapping him on the shoulder. "How's it going?"

"Can't complain," Jim said easily. "Doesn't do any good anyway—nobody listens. How about you?"

"Not much. Julie's out on her first date. She's all excited." Gene laughed. "I think Barbara's more worried about it than the kid."

"You should've brought her along."

"I wanted to, but she said she'd rather stay home."

"Where'd they go?" Jim asked.

"To the Mountain Theater. There's a Halloween thing."

Jim nodded and got up to bowl.

"Okay, guy," Gene yelled encouragingly. "Plenty of headpin… We need a couple of marks to close it out."

Jim's delivery was smooth, but the ball came up high, leaving the three-ten baby split.

"No sweat," Gene yelled. "Easy pickup, babe. Easy pickup."

If Jim missed the split, the team's lead would be cut to about ten pins. Gene looked up at the overhead scoring device and did some quick mental math. They were now ahead by twenty-three pins. They'd lose sixteen or seventeen if Jim failed to convert the split. That would make the match a lot tighter.

Jim approached the lane from the extreme left-hand corner. He walked toward the three-pin and delivered the ball from the left of the center of the lane. The ball was heading to the right of the three-pin. Halfway down the alley, it began to hook back to the left. The ball caught the three-pin on the right side and knocked the ten-pin on the left side.

Jim picked up the baby split.

"Beautiful shot!" Gene yelled. But his praise was drowned out by the applause of his teammates.

Gene followed Jim's split with two strikes in the tenth, putting the icing on the cake. They won the first game by thirty-seven pins.

Gene congratulated his teammates. "I'm buying," he said.

"We've got time while they set up for the second game. Come on over to the bar and give me a hand."

They walked to the bar diagonally across from their lanes. Jim ordered the beers while Gene glanced up at the TV.

Gene wasn't much for TV, but he recognized Robert Wagner and Eddie Albert on the screen. He was watching Switch.

Gene paid for the beers and started back toward the lanes.

Suddenly, the TV screen went blank.

The announcer's voice cut in.

"We interrupt this program to bring you a special bulletin."

Gene turned back toward the TV.

"Reliable sources have just informed this news station," the announcer said solemnly, "that a group of terrorists has taken over the Mountain Theater in Woodland Hills and is holding the patrons hostage."

Gene spilled half the beer, setting the tray on the bar.

The announcer continued, "We have no further details at this time, but we will update this bulletin as we receive more information. Repeating the special bulletin—terrorists are holding several hundred people hostage in a theater in Woodland Hills..."

Gene didn't wait to hear the rest.

He didn't take the time to change into his street shoes.

He raced through the bowling alley toward the parking lot.

It took him two minutes to run from the bowling alley to the parking lot, open the car, get inside, start the engine, and speed onto the street.

He wasn't even aware that he was doing sixty-five miles an hour on surface streets.

Gene knew Barbara was home alone. If she heard the same bulletin... He was afraid of what he might find. Emotionally, his wife was not strong. She was no stranger to hysterics.

Gene slammed the accelerator.

He made a hard right turn, tires squealing as he reached the approach ramp to the Ventura Freeway.

Now that the initial shock had passed, Gene cursed the savagery of the crime.

What was this world coming to?

Just last week in a San Francisco suburb, he recalled, cops and treasury agents had broken into a suburban home in a counterfeiting raid. Six people died. Two of them were cops.

The week before in D.C., terrorists had taken over an office building and held hostages. Miraculously, only one person was killed.

Gene wondered what made people like that tick.

He shook his head and cursed, shifting into the number one lane.

Traffic was light.

Gene floored the gas pedal and watched the speedometer needle shoot up to eighty-five.

Julie's gentle face flashed in his mind.

She was sweet. Innocent. So kind. So happy. So young.

She loved and protected everything—animals and people.

Only last week, she had come home with a stray kitten and begged until Barbara and Gene finally agreed to let her keep it. Tabatha had already become the family mascot.

Fear built up inside Gene's chest.

He was a mile from his exit.

He eased the Continental into the right lane.

A horrible nightmare was beginning.

Less than a quarter of a mile to the exit.

He braked lightly as he hit the off-ramp.

There was a stop sign at the bottom of the ramp—but not for Gene.

Barely glancing to his left, he hit the gas.

The rear end of the heavy Lincoln burned rubber as he gunned the car north on Topanga.

Two minutes later, he was home.

The front door was open.

Gene raced inside.

Barbara was seated on the living room sofa, crying.

But she appeared far more composed than he'd anticipated.

Jill, one of their closest neighbors, sat beside her.

Gene sighed. At least he had that to be thankful for.

He knelt beside his wife, wrapping a reassuring arm around her.

Barbara's body trembled as she sobbed.

He wanted to comfort her.

But there wasn't much he could do.

He wanted desperately to assure her that everything was going to be all right.

But first, someone had to assure him.

8:15 P.M.

THE TRAP CLOSES (GUNMEN MOVE IN)

For some reason, it seems that those directly involved are always the last to know. That was the case at the Mountain Theatre on October 31—Halloween night.

Everyone else had already been informed. People across the state knew. People around the country knew. People in other nations undoubtedly knew. But the hostages themselves—the people being held prisoner—were only now about to learn their fate.

A masked man stepped confidently down the center aisle of the theatre. He climbed the side stairs to the stage. As he reached center stage, the screen went dark, and the stage lights suddenly came alive.

"Look, Mother!" Linda said excitedly, grabbing and shaking her mother's shoulder. "It's the Lone Ranger!"

June put her arm around her daughter and smiled. "Yes, dear," she said. "He's probably going to tell us about the costume contest." She patted her daughter's hand. "Let's listen to him."

Her daughter nodded obediently, sat up straight, and gave her undivided attention to the Lone Ranger.

The Lone Ranger stood proudly at center stage. He was dressed as the famous masked man, complete with a black mask and hat. At his sides were a matching pair of six-shooters. His boots were authentic. But on closer inspection, two things gave him away as a fraud. One telltale sign was the extra fifteen pounds he carried. The second? The bogus hero carried no silver bullets.

Julie and Bryan sat comfortably in the center section, about halfway between the stage and the lobby. Julie held Bryan's hand loosely, growing more confident as the evening progressed.

Julie marveled at the realism of the Lone Ranger's costume. "Pretty neat," she said to Bryan enthusiastically.

Bryan nodded. "I'm looking for Tonto!"

Julie giggled.

"I wonder what he did with his horse," Bryan teased, hoping for another laugh. But Julie was too busy staring at the Lone Ranger.

John Huffington was also staring at the Lone Ranger. Finally, shaking his head, he turned and glanced at his date.

"What's the matter?" the redhead asked softly. "Doesn't he have a permit to carry those things?"

"Very funny," John said, running a finger along her cheek. "He's carrying something... just behind the six-gun on the right side. I can't quite make it out."

The young woman squinted. "I don't see anything."

"Put your glasses on," John said.

"I don't wear glasses."

"Maybe you should."

She punched his arm playfully. "Seriously, I don't see anything."

"Look at his right side," John pointed. "You see the six-shooter?"

"Of course."

"Just behind the six-shooter."

"Oh. That. Now I see."

"What is it?"

"I don't know," she admitted. "I'm not Tonto."

You're not too damned bright, either, John thought, making a mental note to cross her off his list. If nothing else, he hoped for a piece of ass so the evening wouldn't be a total loss.

John closed his eyes for several seconds, leaning back against the headrest.

He saw himself stretched out on the floor of the apartment, pistol aimed at the cat, which had long since disappeared. The prune-faced old lady was hovering over him.

John blinked several times, trying to erase the vision.

The redhead looked at John and decided she wanted his attention. She reached for his hand and placed it in her lap. "You know what I think, Daddy?" she said. "I think those are his extra bullets."

John wasn't sure if she was serious.

"Even the Lone Ranger's bullets aren't that big," he said facetiously.

And he made another mental note—to arrest her on sight if he ever saw her walking down the street. He could charge her with indecent exposure.

John wondered why he found fault with every broad.

They were either stupid and stunning, bright with bad bodies, just plain all-around ugly, had too much ass and not enough class, too old, too young, married, engaged, going with somebody, or engaged in a profession considered immoral or unethical by the department.

John laughed to himself.

Maybe the fault was his.

Maybe he was too picky.

Maybe he should find a plain Jane and settle down.

John shocked himself with that thought. Where the hell did that come from?

Maybe that time would come, but not just yet.

He was too young. He had too much going for him. Too many adventures to pursue before getting tied down.

John slid his hand out of Gloria's grasp, deliberately letting it fall onto her thigh.

What the hell, he thought, his fingers crawling.

John pretended he was with the blonde in the Cadillac.

On stage, the Lone Ranger cleared his throat again.

"Good evening, ladies and gentlemen," he began, smiling. "We'd like to take this opportunity to welcome you to the Mountain Theater and the first annual Halloween Horror Show."

The masked man stood with one hand resting on his six-gun.

"I know it's very dark," he continued, "but we'd like to take this time to make some introductions. For reasons which we'll explain later, it's extremely important that you meet... well, I guess you could call them our team. So let me start by introducing them."

"First, if you'll look to the rear of the theater, to your left. Standing by those doors, you'll see Tonto."

The silence in the theater was interrupted by cheers, applause, and catcalls from kids of all ages.

When the cheers and jeers finally died down, Tonto held his hand up to ward off the Lone Ranger. "Kimosabe," he said, "back to you."

"Thank you, Tonto."

Again, all eyes focused on the Lone Ranger. "Now, if you will," the Lone Ranger said, "at the double doors in the center aisle is Wild Bill Hickok."

Heads turned, and all eyes focused on a figure standing at the back. The man wore authentic Western regalia, complete with a hat and guns. He, too, was somewhat overweight, but the Western wear, slightly large, hid his excess baggage.

Kids applauded loudly. A handful of adults joined in. While Wild Bill's ego was growing with the applause, the Lone Ranger stood rooted to the stage, deeply entranced in thought. All 295,714.28 of them. That was to be his share of the payoff—if they succeeded.

When the cheers subsided, the Lone Ranger again took command. "The last introduction I want to make at this time," the Lone Ranger said, "is the gentleman standing near the center doors, to the rear, your left."

All heads turned. Maverick took off his hat and exaggerated a bow from the waist. For the third time, the theater erupted in cheers and applause. The Lone Ranger sneaked a glance at his watch. Only a couple more hours, and they could all be very, very wealthy—or behind bars.

With each passing minute, the Lone Ranger grew more confident. When this caper had first been suggested, he had had a good belly laugh. It was ridiculous, insane. It might make a good TV movie or a paperback thriller. But that was where its relationship to reality died. The weirdos of this world had pulled some winners, but this would be the one to end all plays.

Nobody would have the balls to attempt something this incredible. Not to mention the manpower and the brains. But then he began to realize that, as far out as it was, it might have potential. Of course, he still had no intention of getting involved. How could he? He, of all people. But the seed, nonetheless, had been planted.

When the reactions and revelry died, the Lone Ranger was aware of the spreading smile on his face. He was thinking positively now. He was thinking about his cut. He was feeling good. The Lone Ranger held up his hand, commanding silence. "Ladies and gentlemen, now you've met three of my dearest friends, let me explain why you have yet to meet the other two. First of all," the Lone Ranger continued, "for reasons which you will learn shortly, Jesse James is in the projectionist booth."

"You will meet him later. Last, and I know you've all been looking forward to meeting this old man of the West—or should I say, this man of the old West—Roy Rogers." There were thunderous "ohs" and "ahs." Dozens of youngsters screamed and applauded. Finally, the Lone Ranger had to hold up both hands for silence. Like good students in his classroom, his pupils obeyed.

While the Lone Ranger hammed it up and kept all minds on the coming show, Maverick leaned against the double doors and thought about his involvement in this incredible scheme. The thing had started at their Tuesday night poker game. Somebody at the table was talking about an actual kidnapping that had been made into a TV movie. A two-man team had kidnapped the daughter of a wealthy Florida man, buried her in a box equipped with a life-support system, and demanded $500,000.

They nearly got away with it. Poor planning got them. Fortunately, the FBI found the girl, and she recovered.

The card clan got to kicking around actual cases. Some argued that the perfect crime was an impossibility. Someone else argued that it could be done, but only under ideal circumstances.

Someone at the table had brought up the famous—or infamous—Willie Sutton. Sutton, aside from being noted for his ingenious, villainous garb, was even admired by some because he never harmed a victim. As a matter of fact, he went out of his way to reassure his victims that they wouldn't be harmed. Willie was almost apologetic. Rumor had it that his weapons were never loaded. He was, to some, a modern-day Robin Hood.

Of course, Willie's clever disguises helped, but you could almost say he had the victim on his side and not be too far from correct.

When he was at large, "The Actor" was one of the most successful, brilliant criminals. And in Willie's entire career, he never hurt anyone—not once.

If this scheme were to have a leader, it had to be the man with the cards in his hand. He was a natural choice. This man was a born leader. "Just for the hell of it," the man had asked, passing the deck to his right to be cut. "If," he continued, picking up the cards, "one of us came up with the perfect crime, you think you'd have the nerve to go for it?"

"Come on, for Christ's sake," Joey said, annoyed at the lousy cards he'd been getting all night. "Are you gonna play cards or screw around?"

"Hang on a minute, turkey. I want to hear more of this," the man with the deck said. "First ace bets," he said.

"Come on," Art goaded. "You're not going to leave us hanging, are you?"

"Bet the ace," the man repeated.

Joey begrudgingly threw a quarter into the pot. "A quarter."

"The idea is plausible," Ernie admitted, calling the quarter. "But how about all the time we'd have to put in? All the planning and whatnot? Not all of us are single," he said, looking directly at Carl. "Some of us are going to have a lot of questions to answer."

The man shrugged, folding his face card. "There's always Tuesday nights."

"True," Carl concurred. He wrapped his knuckles lightly against the table. "Pot, right?" He dealt the cards.

"All I know," Joey said, "is that it would have to be one hell of a plan for me to risk everything."

The man looked at Joey squarely. The contempt he held for the weaker man was evident. "I don't think any of us here are looking to get caught, Joey. None of us wants to spend 5 to 10 years behind bars. Got the idea?"

Joey shrugged but remained silent.

"Yeah," Carl argued, "and your risks are a helluva lot less than mine, too."

Ernie looked across the table. "Call the ace-ten and raise a half." He tossed two quarters into the pot. "Just because I don't have a wife and four kids," Ernie said, "doesn't mean that I don't have just as much to risk as you. It also doesn't mean," Ernie continued, "that deep down in your gut you're not just as big a crook as all of us. Let me tell you something, Mr. Self-Righteous. When it comes right down to it... when all is said and done, we've all got our price. Even you."

Carl started to say something, but Ernie kept talking. "It may not be money, it may be something entirely different, but everyone's got a price... Someday, you just might have the misfortune to find out what yours is."

Ernie looked at Carl. "Bet or drop, damn it," he said contemptuously.

Tonto threw his cards onto the table. "I'm out."

Maverick was suddenly brought back to reality as he heard the Lone Ranger's footsteps on the stage stairs. He looked up in time to see Woody Woodpecker scampering across the screen.

Searching under his coat, Maverick pulled out the walkie-talkie. He held it close to his mouth. "M to L.R.," he said. "What's up?"

The Lone Ranger was walking up the far aisle. He reached behind his six-shooter and pulled out a similar-looking walkie-talkie. "L.R. to M. Go."

"What's happening?"

L.R. keyed the mic. "Nothing," he said. "I just thought the troops might enjoy cartoons. No reason to shake them up yet." The Lone Ranger took a breath. "The show must go on."

9:25 P.M.

SWAT SURROUNDS

Tony Dangerfield drove the unmarked car into the parking lot. He parked head-on in front of the restaurant. Leaving his unlit cigar in the ashtray, TD, as he was sometimes called, checked his watch. 9:23. Less than three hours.

TD exited the car. Slamming the door, Tony walked into the deli. It was dimly lit. Tony checked the counter. No Chief. Tony was about to take a seat at the counter and order coffee while he waited, but at that moment, a girl's voice caught his attention. He turned toward the voice. The teenage cashier pointed to the back of the restaurant, explaining that Tony's party was already seated. As he slid into the back seat, he nodded to the Chief.

Ray Boston, "Sugar Ray," as his friends had nicknamed him, rubbed at the stubble on his chin. Sugar Ray nodded.

"Anything?" Ray asked.

Tony sighed. "I went over every inch of the area. The entire parking lot. No way we can get in... not unless you want to drop a bomb. It just can't be done."

"Okay. Tell me what can be done."

Tony continued confidently, "What can be done has been done. I've got black-and-white and uniformed men blocking off the four corners."

The Chief nodded.

Tony went on, "I'm barricading the streets. This will free more men. I've got SWAT teams on the theater roof and marksmen on the other buildings. I'm saving my own team for the last."

"The bitch," TD said, "is that the entire east side of that theater is brick. There isn't a single piece of glass. You'd think that would be a fire hazard," Tony added. "All the glass is on the north and west sides of the building. Anything we can see from the outside, they can see from the inside. There's virtually no place in the parking lot to put a marksman. It's all concrete and roadway."

"How about the roof of a car? Or better still," the Chief thought out loud, "how about a panel truck? We could put men inside the truck," the Chief suggested tentatively.

Like growing a tree in cement, Tony thought contemptuously. "You could," Tony frowned, "but you're only spinning your wheels. You're not about to fire at that building, and you know it!"

"Relax, Tony," the Chief said. "I'm just thinking out loud. I've been up against some rough ones before, but this tops 'em all. I think I know what it's like to have your hands cuffed behind your back while somebody attacks your wife. It's frustrating as hell." Chief Boston swallowed hard. "I guess we can only wait. I guess the next move is theirs."

Tony reached inside his jacket pocket for a cigar. The Chief was both right and wrong. They had already made a demand. Two million dollars' worth. No response had yet been made to that demand. So, in a sense, the game was still a scoreless tie.

"Okay," Tony said after a long pause. "Let me give the troops a holler and see what's going on. I also want to get my cigars." Tony stood up.

Five minutes later, Tony returned.

"Question," the Chief said as Tony sat down. "What about the bystanders? Any problems?"

"Not really. Not yet. I'd say there are fewer than a hundred right now. We're trying to keep them back, but until the area is barricaded, there's not a helluva lot we can do. I've got men making announcements, pleading with the people, but you know how much good that does. There hasn't been an incident yet. There must be a lot of kids in that theater. From the little we've got, that Halloween show was also a costume party—a family thing. So, I imagine that a lot of the onlookers are scared parents, not bloodsuckers. Whatever you do, you're not gonna turn them away. And I don't blame them. If my kids were in that theater, I'd be out there too."

Tony thought for a moment. "Those guys in there are clever, Chief. They know what they're doing. They're pros."

Ray Boston nodded.

"There's plenty of press out there, too, Boss. Reporters, camera crews. The usual."

Tony held up a cigar with his right hand. With his left hand, he placed a walkie-talkie on the table. He looked at the Chief, sensing that he had something on his mind—something that he was keeping to himself. Tony frowned.

The Chief shook a finger at Tony. "Between the theater," Sugar Ray began slowly, "and the restaurant on the east side, and the bar east of that and that amusement park to the south, how many cars would you estimate are in the lot?"

"Oh, shit," Tony said. "I don't know. If Cal Worthington wanted to start another business in the Valley, this would be the place." Tony blew clouds of smoke toward the ceiling. The waitress set down two coffee cups.

"What's your point?" Tony asked, doing some figuring on a napkin.

"First, give me your figures."

Tony poured cream and sugar into his coffee. "Shit," he mumbled out loud after less than a minute. "There's got to be hundreds of cars by the bar alone." Tony sipped his hot coffee. "Nine to twelve hundred," Tony said finally. "But don't make a book on that. It's illegal."

The Chief nodded. "Tell O'Ryan to get three uniformed men. Let him use his discretion in deploying them. But I want the plate number of every goddamn vehicle in that lot recorded. He can exclude official cars. But anything else that moves—record it. If his men finish that before next month," Chief Boston continued sarcastically, "have someone run the plates through the DMV. One of the girls at the station can handle that. Maybe we'll get lucky."

"The entire lot?" Tony asked incredulously.

"The entire lot," the Chief said. "Every goddamned car, truck, motorcycle, or bicycle."

Tony reached for the walkie-talkie.

"I doubt," the Chief explained after Tony had finished giving Hans the directions, "our boys would be stupid enough to use anything but stolen vehicles. But if we can pinpoint a hot car, we can stake it out. It might be an angle."

Tony agreed with Ray's logic. It was sound. Tony scolded himself for not having thought of it. But that was part of why Ray Boston was Chief, and Tony was into the bookmakers.

"What else you got?" the Chief asked, interrupting Tony's musing.

"I got Gurnsey going through building plans. He used to be in construction. I don't think that's gonna do us any good either, but it's better than sitting on our hands. When you come right down to it," Tony said disgustedly, "there's no way of getting inside the building without risking hundreds of lives."

The Chief agreed. "How about the roof?"

Tony said, "Even Santa Claus couldn't get down the chimney. Believe me. We do have men deployed there... just in case."

Tony sucked on his cigar. "As I see it, you've got three choices."

"Go," the Chief said.

"A: Refuse to give in to their demands. B: Storm the theater. C: Give them their two million."

"Okay," the Chief said. "Leaving A alone for a minute, suppose we opt for B."

"Is that a question?"

"Let's just say I want your input."

"It's gonna get messy as hell," Tony said. "We don't even know what part of the theater they're in or how many of them there are. For my money," Tony concluded, "it's a bad bet."

"I'll go along with that," the Chief concurred. "Then, supposing we go with A. Supposing we just tell them no dice. We ain't playing ball."

"Then the next move is theirs," Tony said.

The Chief faced Tony squarely. "If you were one of those kidnappers inside that theater, and we refused to meet your demands, what would you do?"

"I'm not," Tony said. "And that's not the point."

"That's precisely the point," the Chief said. "What would you do?"

Tony fingered the cigar. "That's an unfair question. I know police procedure."

"You're stalling."

The Chief was right. He had Tony where it hurt.

"I'd have to take a stand," Tony admitted. "I'd have to prove that I meant business."

"And just how do you suppose you'd do that?"

"I'd threaten to kill a hostage."

"And if we still didn't meet your demands?"

"I'd toss you a hostage. Dead."

"Exactly," the Chief said. "Now suppose," he continued, "you aren't one of the kidnappers. Suppose you're a parent of a kid inside that theater?"

Tony thought for a moment. "I get your point. And it's more than valid. But my thinking wouldn't change. You can't pay them."

The Chief was shaking his head. "I can't believe that, Tony. I really can't buy that. Not coming from you."

"Let's forget the eulogy, boss. As far as you and a lot of other people are concerned, fortunately, the decisions are not mine. I wouldn't pay. Period."

"I can't do that, Tony. I can't risk those lives. I just can't do it."

"I understand," Tony said. And then he spat out sarcastically, "Particularly since it's an election year."

There was a long silence.

"Let me ask you a question," Tony said, breaking the silence. "Since it's obvious that it's coming to that... where's the money gonna come from? Who's gonna ante up? You're not talking about the kind of bucks that can be taken out of some emergency fund. You're talking two million dollars!"

The Chief shrugged. "Let's worry about that when we come to it."

"Who have you been in contact with?" Tony asked.

The Chief hesitated.

"The mayor," he said dryly.

"The mayor," Tony repeated evenly. "That puts the fucking frosting on the cake."

The Chief stared at Tony. He said nothing.

"Now listen to me," the Chief said, raising his voice noticeably. "I know what you think of Mayor Franklin, and I don't really care. This is not some high school debating class."

The Chief took a deep breath and squeezed the bridge of his nose.

"If the mayor decides to take over the entire operation, Tony, it's his prerogative. And furthermore, you're going to follow his orders. Like it or not. Is that clear?"

Tony mumbled, "It's clear. But I don't have to like it."

"Just bear this in mind. It's his ass on the line too."

"Who are you kidding?" Tony erupted. "In the first goddamned place, it's an election year. In the second place, he doesn't know police work from baling hay. Take his book away from him, and he couldn't cross the street without getting hit. And in the third goddamned place, the only reason he ever got where he's at is because of his color."

"And in the fourth goddamned place," the Chief spat back, "he's the mayor. I'm the Chief. And it's going to be principles before personalities. Period. Is that clear enough, Tony?"

"And I'm the odd man out," Tony cut in.

"Come on, Tony. Knock it off. You know better. There's a chain of command. I might not like it any better than you. And yet," the Chief sighed, "I honestly don't know that I'd have any other choice if I were running the show."

Then he added, "I don't think I'm going to be running it for long."

"I can't see where we have any other option."

"I don't know about you," the Chief said, "but I've gone a little bit further in my thinking. I'm assuming," he continued, sipping his black coffee, "that we're going to give in to their demands."

Tony was shaking his head. "You're personally gonna give them two million dollars?"

"I don't see any other way out for the hostages."

"I'll tell you what," Tony said dryly. "I wouldn't plan on taking the family to the movies for a while."

"Tony. If we pay them, how are they going to get out of the

theater?"

"I've got a better question," Tony asked. "How are we going to stop them?"

The Chief sighed, staring into his cup. "Do your job, Tony. And we should have them locked in. If we put a net around the area, we've got to get them."

"In other words," Tony deduced, "we're now assuming that you gave them their two million?"

"That's a fair assumption," the Chief stated flatly. "Now answer my question. Assuming they manage to get out of the theater with the money, how are they going to get out of the area if we've got a net around it?"

"The same way they got the two million bucks," Tony shot back.

"They're going to grab a couple of hostages. They're going to walk out of the theater. They're going to hang onto those hostages, get into somebody's car, and take off. And if we even attempt to follow, they'll probably litter the street with bodies. You can't have it both ways. Once they're out of the theater," Tony continued, "you can kiss two million bucks goodbye."

"I'll tell you something, Tony," the Chief said, not hiding his hostility. "I'd rather give them two million dollars and let them walk out with half a dozen hostages than not give it to them and let them hold 500 hostages."

The Chief clenched his fist, slamming it on the table. The

coffee cup almost bounced out of the saucer.

"Has any attempt been made?" Tony asked. "To get the money together?"

"I talked to the mayor," the Chief said. "He's up north. But he's doing what he can. He did say he'd be down as soon as he could get away."

Tony signaled the waitress for more coffee. Both men sat in silence, each wrapped up in his own private thoughts, yet sharing a common concern. Five hundred lives and two million dollars.

As the waitress poured the coffee, she said to Chief Boston, "There's a phone call for you, sir. You can take it behind the counter. The phone's by the register."

The Chief nodded, thanked her, and slid out of the booth.

9:20 P.M.

INSIDE THE PRESSURE COOKER (HOSTAGES)

Sid Highland tried in vain to wipe the sweat from his face. Forcing his shoulder to his cheek with his hands bound behind his back caused a throbbing pain in Sid's shoulder. His arms began to ache.

Sid cursed. He still didn't want to let himself believe that this was happening. Sid was still waiting to be gently shaken awake. He leaned his head against the wall and closed his eyes.

Sid tried to figure out the time. It seemed like he'd been sitting on the floor of the office for hours. And no matter how he tried, Sid couldn't get into position to see his watch. Every time he made the attempt, he only succeeded in tearing more skin off his wrists. The throbbing was now beginning to ease. His wrists were starting to burn and sting. It was bearable. But Sid knew it was going to get more intense before long. Maybe he'd wake up!

Sid looked over at Vince, his young assistant. The kid, as Sid called him, seemed cool and in control. Of course, Sid thought. The kid was too young to realize the seriousness of the situation. Too cocky. Why the hell had they given him such a young assistant anyway?

"Vince," Sid whispered to his assistant. "Vince."

Vince looked at his boss, but he remained silent.

"Vince. What do you think is happening out there?"

Very intelligent question, Vince thought. How the hell should I know? I'm in the same boat you're in.

"I can't tell," Vince said. "I've been trying to listen. But I can't hear a sound. Nothing. I don't understand it." Vince concluded.

"What do you think they want with us? What do you suppose they'll do?"

Vince could see the first signs of hysteria in his boss's face. The son of a bitch wasn't made of ice after all. He was starting to thaw, and Vince had a burning desire to bust Sid's balls some. He owed him at least that. But then he'd be playing Sid's game. Kick 'em when they're down. Besides, there were others involved. A lot of others.

Vince bit his lower lip. "I don't know what they want," Vince said to Sid, aware though that the others could also hear. For that reason, Vince selected his words carefully. "I'm sure once they get what they want, they'll let us go. There's no reason to do anything to us," Vince reasoned logically. "We can't even identify them."

Vince's logic was sound, Sid decided. It made good sense. Once they had what they wanted, they'd have no reason to hurt anyone. Why compound the felony? Sid almost choked on his own pun.

Vince looked down at the floor. Now that he had reassured Sid, what about himself? He wasn't really convinced that they wouldn't be harmed. Hell, anyone crazy enough to pull a stunt like this was capable of anything. Anything.

Vince took a deep breath. He tried to remember whether the penalties for kidnapping and murder in California were the same. He did remember that the death penalty had been restored in California. But did kidnapping carry the death penalty? No, it didn't, Vince decided. The Chowchilla School Bus Kidnapping. Those guys got life, and one of them got off with a lighter sentence.

Now Vince remembered clearly. Something like bodily harm had to be inflicted before the death penalty could be applied. Somehow, Vince wished the penalty were more severe. It might help his chances.

Vince looked at the girls. He tried to smile reassuringly. They appeared relatively composed. As calm as could be expected. Under the circumstances, Vince thought, they were doing quite well. At least they weren't ready to flip out like holier than thou over there.

Vince looked at the ushers. They, too, seemed to be holding their own. That was a good sign. Vince wondered about the theater. He hoped to hell those people didn't panic. It could easily turn into a grisly scene if they lost control. If only one person lost his cool, Vince knew that the whole theater could erupt in seconds. The thought was sickening.

Vince thought of every possible way out. Nothing was going to work. His life wasn't the only one at stake. Vince had the others' lives to consider. He could gamble with his life. That was his business. But not with their lives. Even if there was something he could do, Vince realized the situation was impossible. They were at the mercy of the kidnappers! There wasn't a damn thing Vince could do. God would handle it His way, not Vince's.

Vince flexed his wrists as much as the rope would permit. He wanted to keep the blood circulating. Vince was very aware of the pain. The rope was biting into his skin. But he couldn't feel any blood.

Vince could cope with the physical pain. He had a high tolerance. It was the not knowing, the uncertainty, that got to him. If he knew what they wanted and when they'd be released, it would change the picture. But that was undoubtedly part of their game plan, Vince reasoned.

Vince looked at Marie. Her head was against the wall, eyes closed. Vince swore if he got out of this—if they got out of this—he'd find the courage to ask her out. He'd tell her he loved her.

Vince put his head against the wall and wondered what the hell time it was.

9:50 P.M.

COUNTDOWN BEGINS (NEGOTIATIONS)

The Chief slid into the booth.

"Now what?" Tony asked.

"The kidnappers called again."

"What now? Did they up the ante?"

"No. They just wanted to remind us that we've got about two and a half hours to come up with the money, that everyone in the theater is okay, and that they're enjoying the show."

"On top of everything else, these guys have a sense of humor," Tony said. "I guess if I were about to become a tax-free millionaire, I'd have a sense of humor too," Tony added acidly.

"Is the monologue over?" the Chief asked.

Tony nodded.

"Good," the Chief set down his coffee cup. "Let's get back to basics. We're running out of time. Any bright ideas?"

"No. But I have a question. Assuming—" Tony corrected himself. "Assuming you and your political pal decide to pay, and assuming our friends split by car, what are we going to do? Give them a police escort?"

"Well," the Chief said, ignoring Tony's sarcasm. "Assuming they leave by car, we'll try to maintain a loose surveillance.

When they free the hostages, we'll move in! We've got more maneuvering room once they're away from the theater if you follow me."

Tony followed Chief Boston's logic, even if he didn't agree.

Tony nodded. "How about old eagle eye in the sky?"

"I'm ahead of you," the Chief said. "We've got three choppers on standby."

10:17 P.M.

ESCALATION (DANGERFIELD DECIDES)

The first picture ended at 10:17. It was at this point that the Lone Ranger decided to inform the patrons of their plight. As dozens of people started for the aisles, the refreshment stands, and the restrooms, the lights came on. The Lone Ranger walked on stage.

Some of the people kept moving, some hesitated, some stopped in the aisles, and some returned to their seats.

In a booming voice, the Lone Ranger asked for everybody's attention. Then he gave them a moment to settle down. "If you will all kindly take your seats," he said. "I have an important announcement." The masked man paused, giving the people time to carry out his instructions.

The Lone Ranger looked at his captive audience. He paused again for dramatic effect. Certain that the right moment had arrived, the Lone Ranger began:

"Some of you may be wondering why we told you before that the refreshment stand would be closed during the first show. Let me explain. You may recall that earlier we told you Jessie James was in the projection booth and that you would meet him later.

"We have him upstairs with the projectionist. For the same reason, we have the refreshment stand closed and the doors chained from the inside. You see, you are all being held hostage." The masked man paused. He had anticipated some sort of reaction at this point. There was only silence. "This is no joke," he continued. "You are our prisoners, all of you."

The Lone Ranger was silent as he again waited for the crowd's reaction.

Several people squirmed in their seats. But there was still relative calm, quiet, and disbelief.

"Perhaps you didn't understand me," the Lone Ranger said. "Or perhaps you still think this is a joke. A Halloween prank. Let me assure you, we are playing for real. I, along with my associates, am holding you for two million dollars in ransom. Not so much when you think about it," the masked man explained, obviously savoring his role. "That breaks down to four thousand dollars a head."

"We've been in touch with the newspapers, television... and the police. We assume that right now they're making arrangements to get the two million dollars together."

The Lone Ranger again paused to let the words register. This time, there was a crowd reaction. But it was still subdued. It wasn't what the Lone Ranger had anticipated.

Julie squeezed Bryan's hand. She kept her eyes riveted on the Lone Ranger. Leaning close to Bryan, Julie whispered, "If that's supposed to be a joke, I don't think it's funny. Some of the kids are going to think he's serious. He's going to scare people."

Bryan forced a laugh. He was one of those who were scared. As far as Bryan was concerned, the Lone Ranger had him convinced. Almost!

Bryan thought about that old radio show, the one his parents had told him about, with the Martians landing on the East Coast. And how people had believed it. Thousands of people had panicked. They thought it was for real.

Bryan tried to believe that this was the same sort of thing. Somebody's idea of a Halloween prank. A sick idea. But still only a prank.

Bryan looked all around him. Nobody moved out of their seats; nobody panicked. They were all waiting for further words from the Lone Ranger.

Bryan patted Julie's hand reassuringly. Unfortunately, there was no one to pat Bryan's hand.

10:10 P.M.

TRAPPED INSIDE (MULTIPLE POV)

Don looked at June, then at the kids. The kids hadn't reacted. Either they didn't understand, or they thought it was part of the show. June tried to remain calm. Even in the dimly lit theatre, Don could see the fear on June's face.

Don wasn't quite convinced. He was still clinging to the faint hope that it was somebody's poor idea of a joke. Somebody should tell them, Don thought, glancing quickly at the kids, that this wasn't April Fools' Day. It was Halloween.

Don put his arm around June. She leaned close. He could feel the stiffness, the tension in June's body. He squeezed her shoulder reassuringly, gently kissing her cheek. And then, for some strange reason, which Don could not fathom, his thoughts turned to the 8:00 a.m. parent conference he had arranged for Monday morning. He wondered whether the Vice Principal would be taking his place.

10:10 P.M.

TUNNEL VISION (DANGERFIELD)

John Ruffington's first instinct was to feel for his gun. It was on his left hip, where it belonged. John caressed it reassuringly.

Typical cop's reaction, John thought, shaking his head at his own paranoia. A practical joke, pulling a Halloween prank, and Kojak here is ready for action. John wondered whether, after 16 years on the force, he'd react differently.

The seasoning was what the veterans called it. A sixth sense. It wouldn't take John long to get there.

He reached over and touched Nancy's cheek.

As strange as it seemed, one person in the audience didn't react. There was no alarm on his face. No fear in the pit of his stomach. There was no knot in his gut. He didn't think it was a joke. He didn't think it was a Halloween prank.

He didn't think.

Danny Knight was perfectly still, his head against the back of the seat.

"Okay," the Lone Ranger continued. "Let me start from the beginning. My associates and I have taken over this theater. All of you are our hostages, but don't be alarmed. We're not going to hurt you.... that is, you'll all be released unharmed, as soon as we get what we came for, which is two million dollars in cash."

"I've introduced almost everybody you need to know. To be sure none of you get any ideas, let me warn you that some of us have killed before. That's fact number one. Fact number two, we have automatic weapons and machine guns. Fact number three," the Lone Ranger pointed to a little girl in the very front row, half asleep, with her head resting on her mommy's shoulder. "If anybody gets any cute ideas," the Lone Ranger said very slowly, "that little girl will get it."

The little girl's mother tried to hold back her sobbing. "Relax, lady," the Lone Ranger said. "I'm sure nobody will live with the consequences of trying anything. They wouldn't want to live with the rest of their lives."

The Lone Ranger inhaled. His eyes scanned the theater, quickly, carefully. Everything seemed in order.

"While you're chewing on that," he began again. "Here's dessert. All the doors are chain-locked. You can't get out. The refreshment stand will remain closed. If you must use the bathroom—repeat—if you can't wait, please raise your hand. You will be escorted. Ladies, that goes for you, too. Let me assure you that we want money, nothing more. So don't be shy."

"Only a few more items and we'll get back to the show. As I've told you, half the world has been notified. So you've got a lot of people working for you. I want to assure you one final time that we don't want to harm you. The chances are excellent that by the time the show ends, at a little after midnight, you'll be free to go." The masked man didn't add, "we'll be two million dollars richer," but the thought was in his mind.

"Are there any questions?"

The crowd remained silent. But heads were turning in all directions. Some looked to the exit doors, confirming what their captors had already told them. Even in the dimness, the chains were visible. Others strained to see the outline of machine guns and the silhouette of the costumed men carrying the automatic weapons.

The young mother in the front row clung to her little girl. A middle-aged man seated behind the mother tried to comfort her.

Julie began to scream. She clamped her hands over her mouth, trying to stifle it. It was too late.

John Huffington unholstered his .357. He squeezed it between his legs, finally burying it under his thigh. Then he said a short prayer.

Don tightened his grip on his wife's shoulder. He wanted to say something soothing to the kids. He wanted them to feel that everything would be alright. He wanted to reassure and encourage them. The words weren't there. They wouldn't come.

Don prayed, not for himself. He prayed for his kids. He prayed for his wife. He prayed for the little girl in the front row.

Two teenagers near the front of the theater giggled nervously.

They were among the last holdouts. They were still sure this was a Halloween hoax.

An elderly man toward the back of the theater started to shake violently.

Two heavy-set middle-aged women seated in front of the old man were crying fitfully. A teenage, long-haired boy, wearing a T-shirt that read, "Cowboys stay on longer," stood up and walked falteringly up the aisle. He had taken less than a dozen steps when he was halted by Maverick.

Maverick put his arm on the boy's shoulder. He could tell the youngster was either stoned or high.

The teenager tried to side-step Maverick. Maverick shrugged his heavy shoulders. He said simply, "Sorry, son," and backhanded the boy across the face. The youngster stumbled backward but didn't fall. Maverick led the boy back to his seat.

Satisfied that the youngster would cause no further problems, Maverick continued to patrol the aisles.

Most of the people saw the encounter with the teenager. If they hadn't been convinced before, they were believers now.

Danny Knight still wasn't a believer. Danny still wasn't convinced.

The Lone Ranger had total control now. "Let's quickly review the situation," he said to his audience. "Since you know you can't escape, you're all going to relax. Sit back and enjoy the show, which will continue shortly."

"If you must use the john, raise your hand. You will be escorted. For tonight, heroism is not part of your vocabulary. If you value human life, forget that word."

"When we get our money, which should be at midnight, you will be released unharmed."

The Lone Ranger paused. "If there are any questions, feel free." The masked man scanned the audience, but there were no questions, only shocked silence.

John Ruffington leaned back in his seat and closed his eyes. He tried to recall everything he'd learned in the academy about the present situation.

All his academy training, all his experience, amounted to exactly zilch. John Huffington was in one hell of a spot. He knew it.

John fingered the barrel of the .357 between his legs. He sighed and looked around. He had been a marksman in the Marine Corps and had also turned in top shooting scores at the academy.

John knew damned well that in a split second, he could take out Tonto, who stood guarding the doors to the right. But he knew what would follow. His instinct and training told him that these men meant business. He might just as well shoot the little girl himself.

John palmed the gun, looking quickly to his right. Frustrated, John turned his back on the man guarding the double doors. He holstered the .357.

Don Pearson leaned across his wife, whispering to the girls. "Listen carefully," Don said urgently. "You've heard exactly what we've heard. You know exactly what we know. We know that as long as we do as we're told, nobody's going to be hurt," Don prayed that this was true. "Pretend you're in school, and the Lone Ranger and his friends are your teachers. You're going to do exactly as they tell you to do." Don was thankful that his daughters were both intelligent and obedient. "Before you know it, school's going to be over for the day."

June looked at Don. She was smiling. Don thought it was uncanny how calm and cool June was. Don felt that they had the Lord on their side. He had to believe that everything was going to be all right.

Don leaned over and kissed June on the cheek. Then he looked up at the stage where the Lone Ranger stood. Don cursed the masked man, who seemed to be enjoying the terror he'd struck in the people in the theater.

10:10 P.M.

SMOKE AND MIRRORS (SWAT RECON)

Tony Dangerfield stood near the southwest corner of Victory and Topanga Canyon Boulevard. His hands were teeped at the bridge of his nose. Tony looked first at his watch, then at the scores of people in front of him.

Completely out of sight, atop the roof of the Mountain Theater, tensely awaiting orders, were a handful of the department's best marksmen. They were L.A.'s feared and famous SWAT team. These expertly trained and highly organized men were hand-picked for their ability to deal with crisis situations. On that roof were eight of the department's best. Tony Dangerfield knew that. He knew that because he had selected the eighth floor atop the building.

Tony also had positioned men on the adjacent rooftops. He didn't expect to be able to use these men, but Tony's Chief wanted it that way.

Two blocks to the north and two blocks to the south, uniformed police diverted traffic. West Valley's 'T' units also diverted traffic along Topanga Canyon Boulevard. The traffic units were ordered to keep back as many people and vehicles as possible. Unfortunately, this action was taken too late—hours too late.

Minutes earlier, Tony had overheard a bulletin on someone's radio. Reporters were estimating more than a thousand people already at the scene. Some were relatives and friends of the hostages inside the theater. Most were curious onlookers. And some were there just hoping for bullets and blood. Unfortunately, as long as they obeyed the police, they were within their Constitutional rights. In disgust, Tony bit off the tip of his cigar and spat it on the sidewalk. Police barricades had been set up in a perimeter around the theater. Temporarily, the crowd had been forced back. But the situation was now more ticklish. News teams were on the scene. TV mini-camera crews were doing live interviews. There was a time, Tony mused, when the news media cooperated. Not anymore. Tony cursed aloud. All this would triple the size of the already swelling crowd.

Angrily, Tony jerked the walkie-talkie from his belt. He held it to his mouth and keyed the mike. "Commander to SWAT Leader," Tony said. "Come in, SWAT Leader."

"SWAT Leader. Go, Commander."

"Tony, Jimmie. What have you got?"

"The wind is north-easterly at about 10 miles an hour."

"Cut the comedy," Tony snarled. But he wasn't angry. Jimmie was just easing the tension atop that roof. One of the most wearing phases of police work was the surveillance. The endless hours of waiting, poised, ready to explode like a firecracker. Then, at the last split second, I had to hold back.

"What are the chances of rain?" Tony asked.

"I don't know about rain," Jimmie said, "But I think I see Halley's Comet. Seriously, boss, my men are in position.

Everything's quiet. Which door do your turkeys come out of? We'll pluck their feathers. Of course, telling the players without a scorecard from up here is a bitch. But we'll manage. Have faith."

Tony had faith. He nodded. "Hang tight."

"10-4," Jimmie said.

"10-4, Que."

Tony walked to the east side of the theater. He looked at his watch. The restaurant across the street will be closing shortly. Tony hadn't bothered to position men on the restaurant roof. He didn't think it necessary.

The Chief had left the decision to Tony. But the Chief felt there should be manpower on that roof. Tony deliberated. If there weren't men on that roof, and something went wrong, Tony would catch flak. If he had men on the roof, that would be one less worry.

Tony again looked at his watch. He had time to make a decision. He wouldn't put men on the roof until the restaurant closed. Tony made a mental note to make a move within the next 20 25 minutes.

Walking slowly past the restaurant, Tony reached for the walkie-talkie. "Commander, to Traffic Control King. Come in, King."

"King to Commander. Go."

"How's the traffic situation?" Tony asked.

"No real problems. Parking places are at a premium. The crowd's growing. A couple of guys are selling coffee and cold drinks." Tony shook his head. This was one of the things that never ceased to amaze him. Hundreds of lives are on the line, and some assholes decide to profit from the situation. "Get somebody to check them for permits," Tony spat into the walkie-talkie. "If they don't have any, book 'em."

"10-4, TCK. Out."

"10-4. Clear," Tony said. He placed the walkie-talkie under his jacket and walked to the entrance of the Seller Scene. What was billed as a lounge, Tony knew, was actually a disco for young people. The parking lot was jam-packed.

The Lounge had a reputation as a classy night spot. A clean place to meet people. Such places were becoming fewer and fewer in the valley. Young people sometimes waited for hours to get inside the Lounge. Tony himself had been there a couple of times. It wasn't Tony's thing. But he respected the people who ran the joint. They ran a clean operation.

Mentally, Tony gauged the distance from the Lounge to the theater. He had to decide whether he wanted SWAT teams on this roof. Tony again estimated the distance. He tasted his lower lip, a signal that he was ready for a cigar. As Tony fired up the cigar, he made a decision.

The Lounge was too far from the theater. No men on that roof. It was a waste of manpower. Tony turned and started back in the direction of the theater.

Tony thought about the horses as he walked slowly from the Lounge to the theater. He wanted to grab a couple of free minutes to check out the form. There was a big turf race at Holly Park tomorrow. Tony wanted to look over the field.

Toro was up on Miss Toshiba. The horse was a hell of a horse. And Tony had made some big bucks on it. But Tony felt this outing might be carrying too much weight.

Miss Toshiba had won its last two starts. But this time, it was not only stepping up in class, but it was also carrying more weight. Tony was anxious to see how much more weight it was going to carry. Depending on the weight and the odds, Tony would then decide on the size of his bet.

He'd already decided to bet on the horse. The question was, how big a bet? If Tony bet a chunk, and the horse came through, Tony would almost be home free. On the other hand, if the horse lost, Tony could be damned near buried again.

Tony stopped in front of the theater. His eyes were drawn to the marquee lights. It read: SPECIAL HALLOWEEN SHOW. Tony thought about the people inside. Then, about the perpetrators. Then, about the horses. Then back to the people trapped inside. Then back to the perpetrators. Then the horses. Then himself. Then he thought, maybe he wouldn't place that bet after all. Even a champion has to lose sometimes.

10:25 P.M.

HOSTAGES STIR (INSIDE TENSION)

Barbara Snow sat on the couch in the living room of their modest home. She stared at the TV. She saw nothing.

Barbara was terrified. She was terrified for her daughter, who was inside the theater. And Barbara was to blame for it all. She shouldn't have let Julie go on that first date. She was too young. Her wrong decision had put her daughter in a situation that might cost Julie her life. Barbara buried her face in her hands and sobbed.

Barbara wasn't aware of the tears trickling down her face. She wasn't aware of sirens screaming nearby. She wasn't aware that her husband was in the bathroom, showering, trying to drain some of the tension.

Barbara's whole world was the TV set. Through tear-streaked eyes, she saw the newscaster walking around the theater parking lot. Barbara knew the scene. She had often shopped across the street from the theater. She saw the newsman interviewing people within feet of the theater. Their reactions all added up to the same:

Terrible. Unbelievable. Tragic.

The cameramen varied their angles. They shot a close-up of a black and white screeching to a halt at the curb, lights flashing a brilliant, urgent red.

"Ladies and gentlemen," the newscaster said, the camera

holding on the black and white. "The West Valley Police Department has asked us to make the following announcement: Those of you who are keeping abreast of the tense situation here at the Mountain Theater, those of you who have friends or relatives inside the theater, those of you who would just like to help, can. We must have your cooperation. We ask you to stay at home and keep tuned to your local television and radio stations for live, on-the-spot coverage."

Barbara leaned forward and stiffened.

"Because of the serious situation at the theater, thousands of people are now on the scene. The situation demands that all manpower be properly used, not wasted on crowd control and traffic directing. We ask you again, please stay at home. Stay tuned to local stations for live coverage. Thank you for cooperating."

The cameras followed four uniformed policemen as they exited the squad car and walked to their traffic post.

Barbara's eyes were glued to the television.

Gene toweled himself dry in front of the full-length bedroom mirror. He thought of his options. He could think of only one: sit still and wait.

Gene could handle that. What he didn't know he could handle was the action the police would take. The next move was theirs. The kidnappers had made their demands. Now the police had to pay or act. Two million dollars was a huge sum of money. But the payoff in itself didn't guarantee the release of the hostages. However, Gene couldn't see these people harming them.

Gene was not a gambler. But he'd lay odds that the police would make the payoff. They'd have to. If they didn't, and anybody in that theater was hurt or, worse, killed, the public reaction would be devastating. Careers would be on the line. And Gene knew damned well that before these politicians risked their careers, they'd come up with the money. He'd bet his life on that. Gene wished it were that simple. He wished it were only his life that was at stake.

10:25 P.M.

BEHIND THE CURTAIN (GUNMAN POV)

Like a soldier on guard duty, the kidnapper garbed as Tonto paraded up and down the far aisle. At Tonto's side, those in aisle seats could make out the outline of a submachine gun.

There was almost total silence among the patrons. You could taste the tension.

A big man, thick-shouldered, slightly heavy-set, and costumed as Wild Bill Hickok, marched in cadence down the center aisle. He, too, carried a black object at his side. John Ruffington was able to identify that object when Hickok walked past.

When Hickok was three feet beyond him, John suddenly let go of his girlfriend's hand. John Ruffington had made a decision.

At that moment, the plainclothes, off-duty cop decided that doing something beat the hell out of sitting on his fat ass, being an observer. John had to do something. He had to make a move. He knew they could all be running out of time.

John reasoned that by doing nothing, he was aiding and abetting the bandits. The longer he sat passively, the guiltier he became.

John glanced to his far left. He could see a figure in black doing an about-face at the bottom of the far aisle. The man in black started back up the aisle.

Maverick also had an object at his side, similar to what the other two kidnappers carried.

By John's arithmetic, there were at least six of them inside the theater. There was the Lone Ranger, apparently in command. Tonto, presently parading up and down the right-hand aisle. Wild Bill Hickok, holding down the center aisle. Maverick, guarding the left-hand aisle. And, as John recalled, the Lone Ranger had said earlier that Jesse James was upstairs with the projectionist. Roy Rogers was either in the lobby or with the theater employees.

John looked all around. A plan was forming in his mind. There were easily three or four hundred people in the theater.

Shit! he mumbled. The odds were 50, 60, or even 70 to one.

There had to be some way to form a plan of attack. Some way to overpower these guys. John was sure that while almost everyone was apparently watching the movie, some of the men in the theater had to be thinking along the same lines as he was.

John was certain that you didn't have to be a cop to want to nail these guys.

Okay, John told himself, calmly and logically. He had to work up a plan of attack. That was elementary.

Don't attack until you have a plan, a blueprint.

John had to organize his thoughts. The first thing he had to deal with was the weapons—their machine guns. But even before that, he reminded himself that he was going to need help. He couldn't take out half a dozen men with automatic weapons by himself. Kojak, he wasn't. A few of his fellow hostages would have to lend a hand.

John looked first to his left, then to his right.

On his immediate left was his date. To her left were a couple of kids. Forget them.

John glanced casually to his right. Two teenagers sat next to him, then a chubby-faced middle-aged man.

But the problem wasn't just taking out Wild Bill Hickok. All he had to do was get past those three people on his right, and he could handle Hickok.

The problem was—once he nailed Hickok, who was going to handle Tonto and Maverick?

And now, there was a further problem John hadn't anticipated.

Where the hell was the Lone Ranger?

Damn. If we don't take out the three of them in one fell swoop, and if one of those jerks gets trigger-happy, there's going to be a bloodbath.

John fingered the hammer of his magnum.

His plan lacked two essentials.

The first was a means of communication.

How the hell was he going to get the attention of people across the aisle from him?

And if John got their attention, then how could he do without the second?

Experience.

These people weren't trained to handle crisis situations.

Would they give John the help he needed?

Would they?

John was now having second thoughts.

If his commanding officer were sitting next to him, what would he do?

Would he decide that the better part of valor was no action?

Would his CO say to think first of the hostages?

Or would he say that, under the circumstances, action was the only option?

John wondered whether his judgment was clouded by being in the middle of the situation.

What was happening went more against John's grain than anybody else's.

John had been trained to react in crisis situations. But this was a unique situation. He wondered what the guys in the locker room would be saying about him sitting there, doing nothing. He wondered how a seasoned veteran would react—someone like Lt. Hedge.

Big Bad John, they'd call him. Big Bad John! Sat there and let it happen. And they'd crack wise behind his back. And Crosby! Crosby wouldn't even have the decency to make remarks behind his back. He'd make them right in front of John. Well, he'd fix him. John made a promise to himself—if Crosby so much as opened his mouth, John would drop him like a bad habit. That is, if he got out of this alive.

Through the dimness, John's eyes slowly, deliberately searched the seats, starting with those at the far right. John wasn't exactly sure what he was looking for. A face that looked like it was tough enough to handle these guys? A face that didn't seem to be as afraid? A face that looked like it wanted to do something?

Two ten-year-olds, a couple of rows in front of John, were pestering their parents. Their voices had grown loud, and John could hear them clearly. They wanted hot dogs, popcorn, and pop, and they kept insisting on going to the refreshment stand.

John watched as a man a couple of rows in front of him stood up and eased his way to the aisle. Out of nowhere, Wild Bill Hickok was on the scene.

John couldn't be sure what the man was saying to Hickok. He guessed he was asking to go to the men's room. Hickok nodded his head. Both men started walking up the aisle.

John ignored the two fights on the screen. The actress had her back to the man holding a knife above her head. John didn't hear her scream as she turned in time to see him slashing down with the knife. John didn't see the screen fill with bright red. He didn't see the woman fall. He didn't see the man plunge the knife into her again and again.

John was giving birth to a plan of attack. His subconscious had labored and ejected into his consciousness the fetus of a developing plan.

John's problem of communication was solved.

He first had to get into the men's room. He had to get a few others in there with him or figure out some way of communicating with people who went into the men's room—without actually being there himself.

John asked himself: If he were to get up and walk to the men's room now, would he be able to talk to the other man? Would he be stopped? If he forced the issue, would Hickok waste him? John was sure he'd get to exchange at least a few words with the guy. Would that be enough?

Obviously, he couldn't get away with running back and forth to the head.

Suddenly, John's eyes opened wide.

You stupid bastard!

John smiled. There it was! It was there all the time, and John hadn't even realized it. What a dummy! Shit! If the guys at the station knew about this, they'd really laugh. But they didn't know. And John could turn it to his advantage.

John was going to get the chance to do what he was sworn to

do.

Now it all came clear. It was simple. Wild Bill had no way of knowing who he was. Hickok had no way of knowing he was an off-duty cop with a .357 under his jacket. All John had to do was wait for the other guy to come back from the head, then ask permission to go himself.

Once he was inside, he'd go into a cubicle. Wild Bill would be waiting outside the cubicle. But he wouldn't be expecting John to come out with a .357 levelled at his belly.

Unfortunately, John had left his handcuffs at home. But he'd manage without them. It wouldn't be John's fault if Wild Bill resisted, and John was forced to hit him. If he hit him too hard, well, wouldn't that be just too bad? He'd be saving the taxpayers money.

Problem number two should be easy enough—take the machine gun from Wild Bill, swap clothing, and stick Wild Bill in the stall. That would reduce the odds. It would then be five to one. But it would also give John an added advantage. They wouldn't know what he'd know. Wild Bill Hickok wouldn't be Wild Bill Hickok. He'd be Wild Bill Ruffington!

The more John thought about the plan, the better he liked it. Come on, asshole, he thought. Hurry up and get your rear end out of the john!

10:45 P.M.

STRATEGY FORMED (COMMAND POST)

Tony Dangerfield looked across the table at the black face. The black face he didn't like. The black face he'd learned to dislike ever since he'd ridden with that face in the squad car years ago. The black face he had so often seen on the front page, both when he was campaigning for office and after he had become mayor. Since that black face had become mayor, Tony had come to despise it. Not for the reasons most people gave. Prejudice had nothing to do with it. Nothing at all.

The few people who knew Tony Dangerfield intimately knew that he was not a racist. As a matter of fact, he despised the mayor for exactly the opposite reason.

Lincoln A. Franklin, or "Laf" as Tony liked to call him, had always "used" his black heritage to his advantage. He'd turned and twisted every situation to make his color work for him. He was one of those who was going to continue to make people pay in spades for past discrimination, long after the debt had been repaid.

Franklin had used it to gain advantages within the department, where advantages supposedly couldn't be obtained. He'd used it to carve his way into politics. He'd used it to climb the political ladder, a rung at a time, and finally, against impossible odds, Franklin used it time and again in his campaign for mayor. When the last votes were in, Tony had a "Laf for mayor."

Tony Dangerfield admired a fighter. He'd go for the underdog almost every time. Tony, without reservation, believed that every man should have equal rights. And he believed that principle should be applied both ways. A man should be treated no better or worse because of his color. Tony sure didn't believe in the argument that, because blacks had supposedly been held back for generations, now they were entitled to special privileges.

Almost all people at one time or another had been persecuted, held back, and shit upon. That didn't mean they were entitled to special privileges today. If we were going to start handing out privileges to people because they had been persecuted years ago, Tony guessed that three-quarters of the United States should rightfully belong to the Indians.

We, as a people, undoubtedly made a lot of mistakes in the past, but the past is still the past. As trite as it sounded, bygones were bygones. You paid your debt and moved on. You had to forgive and forget. Yesterday's society was not today's. Tony didn't see any reason to pay off yesterday's debt at today's interest rate. It didn't wash.

Because Mexicans, blacks, and Puerto Ricans had it rough yesterday didn't mean that for every white hired, three Mexicans and three blacks also had to be hired. If they earned it, fine—but make them earn it. As far as Tony was concerned, nobody was entitled to preferential treatment.

That was equal rights, as Tony saw it.

Within the department, there was room only for the best. Give somebody a little wedge to pry pebbles free, and before you know it, rocks are falling, and then there's a landslide—all because you allowed that lousy little pebble to be moved. In Tony's mind, that was a Laf!

A man who never possessed the tools to be a good cop was given a wedge. That wedge worked once. So, to that man's way of thinking, it could work again. And it did—again and again and again.

The rule of the Peter Principle popped into Tony's mind. His Honor, the mayor, had climbed not to his level of incompetency, but above it. As far as Tony was concerned, Laf had been an incompetent cop to begin with. Now he was an incompetent mayor.

But worse than that, Tony was sitting across the table from him. And with 500 lives at stake, Tony would have to work with the man. With two million dollars at stake, Tony would have to listen to His Honor's bullshit. And, damn it, Tony would have to toe the mayor's line.

Tony reached into his pocket for a cigar. He'd put one out only minutes ago. He really didn't want another one. But knowing His Honor detested cigar smoke, Tony fired up, blowing the smoke in the mayor's direction.

"I'm sorry we have to meet again under these unpleasant circumstances, Tony..." the mayor started.

Tony didn't let him finish the sentence.

"I'm sure it could be worse," he said.

He wanted to add that I could be back in the squad car with you. I could be riding with you day after day. But Tony kept his mouth shut. He knew, as close as he and the Chief were, there was a chain of command. And if Tony smart-mouthed the mayor, he could issue the order, and the Chief would have no choice. The axe would drop. And along with Tony's neck would go his pension.

So Tony swallowed his pride and ate the words he wanted to spit out. He sighed, blowing more smoke across the table. He was certain the mayor got the idea.

"Okay," the mayor said, deliberately looking first at the Chief, then at Tony. "Since I've taken official command of this investigation, will one of you fill me in on the details?"

Stiffly, Tony gave Mayor Franklin the facts. Where the Chief thought it necessary, he cut in.

"And that's it, up to the minute," Tony said, flicking ashes into the ashtray.

The mayor looked at his watch. "We've got till just after midnight?"

"That's it," Tony nodded.

"Okay," the mayor said after a brief silence. He looked directly at Tony. "How do you suggest we handle it?"

"I'm not in favor of paying them if that's what you—" Tony

said.

"I think the question was quite clear," the mayor shot back. "I didn't ask you what you were not in favor of. I asked you what you suggest we do."

Tony blew a huge cloud of smoke across the table. "I suggest we tell them we can't come up with that kind of money."

The mayor shot back, "Keeping in mind your valuable training, your many years of experience, Detective Dangerfield, just what the hell do you suppose they'll do if we refuse to meet their demands?"

"I don't think we can answer that question," Tony said. "It's just speculation at this point."

"Why don't you try using your imagination? Your professional judgment?"

Tony shook his head. "I'd rather not deal in imagination."

The mayor cut in. "I don't want to deal in imagination either. I want to deal with the reality of human lives—500 of them!"

"So you're going to give them their money?"

"I'm going to do whatever's necessary to gain the safe release of those hostages."

Tony bit down on the cigar. "What the hell is that supposed to mean?"

"That means we'll meet the ransom demand. But it also means," the mayor said, jabbing a finger toward Tony, "that you'll come up with some sort of plan." The mayor waved his hand in the air. "Some plan of attack... some..." He searched for the right word. "Some maneuver to keep them from getting away once they've released the hostages."

"Just like that," Tony said sarcastically. "Maybe you've got a cape around somewhere with a big S on it that I can borrow."

"Look," the mayor said pointedly, ignoring the Chief's facial expression. "I'm not saying you're going to do something that will prevent them from getting away or from making good their escape after we've given them the money or after they've released the hostages. I am saying that you are going to try. My main concern is the safe release of every one of those hostages. I happen to believe that they don't want to hurt anybody. And I don't think they will, as long as we meet their demands. I do think that they are prepared to spill blood if we don't meet their demands. And frankly, I don't intend to risk that."

"Yeah. It is an election year," Tony said, half under his breath.

"That's got nothing to do with it, Dangerfield."

"' Course not," Tony said sarcastically. "I know you wouldn't use a wedge like this to your advantage. I was just stating a fact. I'm sure it's only incidental to you that this is an election year."

"Enough, Dangerfield," the mayor yelled, slamming his fist on the table. "I've had enough—all I'm going to take. If you want to continue with this investigation, Dangerfield... and let me add, if you enjoy police work and want to continue, I suggest you stop giving me a hard time." The mayor's voice underscored the last two words.

A cloud of smoke drifted across the table, hanging in the mayor's face.

"You made yourself quite clear," Tony hissed through the smoke.

The mayor sat back, silent, until the smoke cleared. Then, "Okay. Here's what we're going to do. I'm going over to the theater. Even though I'm sure it won't do any good. I'm also sure it won't do any harm. I'm going to try to get one of the kidnappers to talk to me."

"What kind of deal are you going to try to make?" Tony demanded.

Softly, almost pleadingly, the mayor asked, "Why don't you give me a break, Dangerfield? If not for me—if we had a choice—then for God's sake, for the people in that theater."

The mayor continued, "None of this would be happening. The three of us wouldn't be here. But since we don't have a choice, and since it is happening, and since we do have to be here... why don't we work together and forget our private differences?" The mayor looked directly at Tony. "We can deal with that later."

"With the three of us giving this our best shot, Dangerfield, those people in there may have a chance. Without us, they're no better than some of the horses you've picked."

The mayor's dark eyes were cold as they stared Tony down.

"Touche," Tony said finally. He knew he had lost the round. But their fucking fight was far from over.

The mayor reached into his shirt pocket, drew out a pack of green, mentholated cigarettes, and lit one. He took two drags, then spoke.

"Now that we understand each other," he focused his attention on Tony, "I'm going to make that call to the theater. I'm going to see if I can get one of the kidnappers to talk to me. I know damned well I'm not about to talk them into surrendering, but I might be able to feel them out. Maybe I can buy more time... or find out what's going on in there. Maybe I can find out if everybody's okay. Maybe they'll let something slip. Who knows? I'll play it by ear."

"But your job," Mayor Franklin said, pointing the cigarette toward Tony, "is much more important. I want you outside the theater, Tony. I want you to canvass every bit of that theater... from the outside, of course. In..." the mayor paused to look at his watch, "...in no more than 25 minutes, I want you to know the layout around that entire area: the parking lot, the bar next door, the adjacent buildings, etc., as well as you know the back of your hand."

Tony looked confused. "Your point being what?"

"My point being..." The mayor sighed. "...that while I have every expectation of giving in to their ransom demand and coming up with the two million bucks, once the hostages are safely released, I think that if you can come up with some plan of attack, we can nail these guys before they get out of the area."

The Chief remained silent.

"Are you keeping something from me, Mr. Mayor?" Tony asked. "Is there something you know that I don't?"

The mayor shook his head.

"I've been over and over that ground," Tony said. "I don't see how we're going to do it. There are four possible exit doors—two on the north side and two on the south side. There's the emergency door in the rear of the theater. That would be the end. Those aren't double doors like the ones on the sides of the theater. Those doors aren't wide enough to accommodate a mass exit of 500 people if they were to let them all out at one time. And I've already figured that that's their best bet.

"The only other option would be for them to come out the front. There's too much glass there. With all the people they've got out front and all the glass surrounding the theater, everybody and their uncle would be able to see the release of the hostages if they used the front. They've got to be looking for the element of surprise. I seriously doubt they'll do that.

"The best bet," Tony said, "would be the double doors on either the north or south side."

"If that's what you think," the mayor said, "keep that in mind when you double-check the area. Maybe you'll come up with something... something you missed."

The trio sat silently, each lost in his own thoughts. Tony's main concern was the mayor's intention to pay off two million dollars. The mayor was concerned with 500 people, two million dollars, and an election year—not necessarily in that order. The Chief was concerned with Tony's insubordination, the 500 people in the theater, several thousand people outside the theater, two million dollars, and his upcoming retirement, which just might come sooner than he had been anticipating.

"Question, Mr. Mayor," Tony asked, rubbing his fingers along the table top. "I take it there's going to have to be an exchange of money before there's an exchange of hostages. If that exchange takes place inside the theater, and if the kidnappers don't stipulate who's to make the delivery, let me be the one to take the money inside."

"Any particular reason?"

Tony nodded. "I may be able to pick up something that could help me on the outside. Like how many kidnappers there are, what kind of weapons they're carrying—any little thing that might help."

The mayor nodded approvingly. "Sounds good to me. Oh, one other thing," he added. "Get me a walkie-talkie. I want to keep as close to the action as possible."

"No problem," Tony said. "As soon as I leave, I'll have one sent over."

The mayor nodded his thanks. "Well," the black man said, "I guess that about does it."

Tony looked across the table. "I've got one other question."

"Shoot."

"How the hell do you deliver two million dollars in cash?" Tony asked.

The mayor stared at Tony.

Tony would have sworn that the mayor's face damned near turned white.

Tony was deadpan.

"You deliver it very, very carefully," the mayor said to Tony, as Tony started to slide out from his seat.

11:05 P.M.

POSITIONING (SWAT READIES)

Before Tony toured the theater area again, he had a walkie-talkie sent to the mayor in the delicatessen.

Tony sat behind the wheel of the unmarked police car. He didn't start the engine. Instead, he marveled at the sheer number of people who had turned out for the occasion.

The crowd had swelled since he'd been in the restaurant. He estimated several thousand people, and he guessed more would arrive shortly. Tony wondered how many had friends or relatives in the theater and how many were just bloodsuckers, as he liked to call them.

He shook his head in disgust. Television and radio appeals had pleaded for people to stay home. They had been told their absence would help the investigation and that their presence would only hinder it. But apathy prevailed.

People just didn't care. They wanted to be in on the action, regardless of the risk to others. Spectator sports had become the thing of the day—the more brutal, the better.

Tony recalled a recent Dodgers game he had attended with his son. It was a night game at the stadium, a hell of a ball game. Jerry Koosman started for the Mets, and Doug Rau was on the mound for the Dodgers. It had been a pitcher's duel well into the late innings.

The Mets had scored first on a homer by Mike Vail. In the

third inning, the Dodgers tied it with a walk, a single, and a Mets error. The score stayed tied until the Dodgers tallied twice in the bottom of the eighth, and that's how it ended—3 to 1.

Tony had enjoyed the game even more because he was with his son, but the crowd's reactions had disgusted him. At one point, a Doug Rau fastball had come in so close to Bud Harrelson that he had to hit the dirt. The fans were disappointed that the ball hadn't hit him.

Later, some jerk in the upper deck tossed a beer in the face of a guy cheering for the Mets. No provocation—only that the man was rooting for the opposition.

Three times, the game had to be stopped because people ran onto the field. Once, the offender was just a kid.

Tony turned the key and started the engine. He put the car in gear and eased his foot down on the accelerator. Two uniformed policemen moved the barricades so he could get the car within a hundred feet of the theater façade.

He drove slowly past the front of the theater. When he reached the brick façade, he slowed down.

Two hundred feet beyond the beginning of the brick facing was the first set of exit doors. Tony maneuvered the car so the headlights focused on them. He flipped on the high beams, put the car in park, set the emergency brake, and got out.

Tony walked up to the iron doors. They were painted rust-red, the high beams lighting them up. Taking nothing for granted, he inspected them carefully.

It took several minutes to complete his examination. When he finished, Tony had a complete diagnosis—and a prognosis. Slowly, he walked back to the car. He continued driving slowly along the side of the building.

He wondered what it would be like to have a share of two million dollars. Think of what you could do with more than that, tax-free.

Tony kept driving, looking and thinking. What would it be like to be financially comfortable? Comfortable enough that he didn't have to sweat property taxes, rising gasoline prices, skyrocketing food costs, tuition hikes, and the ever-increasing price of clothing?

He was getting fed up with watching his wife budget for food. It had gotten to the point where she was even trying to cut back on coffee.

Tony was a coffee drinker.

Well, Tony thought...

Something snapped him back to reality. He checked his watch. They were running short on time.

It was 11:15.

Less than an hour to come up with the money.

Tony focused his eyes on the side of the building. Less than an hour.

He wondered how the mayor had made out with his phone call.

He wondered what was going on inside the theater.

Tony could feel the tension creeping inside him.

"This is the mayor, Tony," came a voice from under the dashboard, startling him. "Do you copy?"

Tony reached for the mic. He keyed it. "I copy. Go."

"Got anything for us?"

"Negative."

"I'm about to make a phone call. Anything special you think I should mention?"

Tony rubbed his lip, coaxing his thoughts. He held the mic to his mouth.

"Yeah. Ask them what time the cartoon goes on."

"10-4," the mayor said. The mic on the other end went dead.

11:10 P.M.

READY TO MOVE (JULIE & BRYAN)

The family doctor stepped out of Barbara's bedroom, pulling the door partway closed. Gene was pacing the living room nervously. At the sound of the doctor's footsteps, he turned quickly, searching the man's face for a sign.

The doctor patted Gene's shoulder reassuringly. "Relax," he said, leading Gene into the kitchen, where they sat down at the table. "She'll be fine. I gave her a sedative. She should sleep through the night."

Gene nodded. "Any chance she'll wake up in the middle of the night?"

The doctor shook his head. "I gave her a strong dose. The emotional strain has already taken a toll. The rest will do her good. Professionally, Gene, Barbara doesn't need any other medical attention—there's nothing else anyone can do now." He hesitated, then added sincerely, "But as a friend, if there's anything I can do… anything at all, don't hesitate to call."

Gene thanked him. As the doctor opened the front door, he turned back. "You have my prayers."

Gene paced the living room floor. The tension was beginning to show on his face. He looked out the front window. The street was deserted. He stared into the darkness, then checked his watch. Less than an hour until the show let out. He walked back into the living room and turned on the TV.

The scene on the screen was all too familiar now. Cameras were still panning the shopping center parking lot across from the theater. At this hour, the lot was usually empty, but now it was crammed with cars. Curious onlookers scurried from the parking lot across the street to the theater, stopping only when confronted by uniformed policemen standing guard at the barricades.

Gene flipped through the channels. Every major network was covering this "special report." It was too much to take. Finally, he shut the TV off.

He walked into the bedroom and looked down at his wife. She lay on her side, appearing to sleep peacefully.

Gene hovered over Barbara. He swallowed hard, choking back tears. He squeezed the bridge of his nose between his thumb and forefinger, but it was no use. Tears streamed down his cheeks. He wondered absently who the tears were for—Barbara, Julie, or himself.

Abruptly, he turned away and walked back to the living room. He began pacing again, then made a decision. He found Mrs. Lyon's phone number in Barbara's desk directory. When she answered, he apologized for the late hour and explained the situation. He asked if she could come over.

Mrs. Lyon had been Julie's babysitter. Gene couldn't leave Barbara alone.

She assured him she'd be over in fifteen minutes. Gene thanked her, hung up, and walked into the bedroom.

As quietly as possible, he searched the closet for a light jacket.

He was sitting on the living room couch, impatiently puffing on a cigarette, when he heard a light knock at the door.

"Come on in, Mrs. Lyon," he said, opening the door wide.

"I'm sorry to disturb you so late, but under the circumstances…"

She cut him off mid-sentence. "Don't say another word. I'm happy to help."

Gene didn't reply. Mrs. Lyon wasn't sure he even heard her. She could only imagine what he was going through.

He led her to the couch. Once she was seated comfortably, he gave her instructions.

"Barbara's asleep in the bedroom. The doctor gave her a shot. She'll probably sleep straight through till morning, but I just didn't want to leave her alone."

Mrs. Lyon nodded. She could see the pain in Gene's eyes, the worry etched into his face. She had never seen him like this before.

"You know where everything is," he continued. "If you want anything, help yourself. If you get tired, you can sleep on the couch. I don't know when I'll be back."

"Do you want to leave a phone number?"

Gene looked down at the older woman. He shook his head.

"I'm going over to the theater. I know there's nothing I can do, but it's better than sitting here. I can't stand the waiting. I just can't take it anymore. At least over there, I'll be closer to Julie. If anything should happen…"

He didn't finish the sentence. He didn't dare.

He double-locked the front door behind him.

11:18 P.M.

NEARING THE END (TENSIONS RISE)

Mayor Franklin held the phone in his sweaty palm, counting the rings. By the twentieth, he stopped. His ear was damp with perspiration, so he shifted the receiver to the other side. Still no answer.

Finally, a voice crackled through the line. "Mountain-Theater."

"This is Mayor Franklin. Who's this?"

"How's Roy Rogers grab you?"

The mayor fingered the cigarette pack in his shirt pocket and took a steadying breath. "Listen to me, please," he urged. "You have absolutely no chance of getting away with this. All you're doing is making things worse. If you give up now, I promise you, things will go a lot easier. I will personally guarantee leniency. Don't make this any harder than it has to be."

A pause.

"Are you finished, Mr. Mayor?"

"Yes. Yes, I'm finished."

"Good," Roy said.

He was half-sitting, half-leaning, his eyes scanning the room of bound employees. His gaze locked onto Vince, lingering. A cocky smirk stretched across his face.

"Now it's my turn," Roy said. He didn't wait for a response. "Let me emphasize what you already know, Mr. Mayor. We have a lot of people inside this theater. As you've been told, we don't intend to hurt them. But we will do whatever the hell we have to do to convince you that we mean business. And trust me—we mean business."

He glanced at his watch. "This show is due to let out just after midnight. We don't have all that much time. So I suggest you get that two million dollars together and get it together fast. I don't think you'd want us to prove that we mean business. That would get messy."

He chuckled. "Look at it from our perspective, Mr. Mayor. Having come this far, wouldn't it be stupid for us to give up now? We're not risking much more than we already have. If anything, the gains outweigh the risks."

Roy leaned forward. His voice dropped to a near whisper.

"We are not amateurs. This has been carefully planned. We hold all the cards… and all the chips. And if that's not enough for you, let me spell it out—the game is rigged in our favor."

His tone darkened. "If you want these people released unharmed, get that two million bucks together. Fast. I don't want to have to say this again. If you try to back us against a wall, we'll prove we mean business. And something tells me you don't want to see that."

A long silence. Then Roy added, almost casually, "Some of us have killed before. And believe me, we're prepared to kill again. But only if you force the issue. If anything happens, Mr. Mayor, it'll be on you. You will pull the trigger. Remember that."

Another pause.

"Now, assuming you've made up your mind about getting the money, here's what you're going to do. Get it all together. Then call me back at this same number. Let it ring three times, hang up, and immediately dial again. That'll be my signal to answer. I'll have further instructions for you then."

The mayor wiped the sweat from his ear.

"Mr. Mayor, any questions?"

The mayor shook his head. "No questions. But I still think you're making a big mistake. If you'd only—"

The line went dead.

Roy cradled the receiver and turned toward the hostages. He would have liked to untie their hands, but he couldn't take the risk.

Facing the girls, he sighed. "Listen, that was Mayor Franklin on the phone. They're getting everything ready on their end. It won't be much longer. I want you to know, I'm sorry you have to go through this. But there was no other way—really, there wasn't."

He watched as one of the young girls struggled to scratch an itch on the back of her neck, twisting her shoulders in frustration. He was about to say something when—

A bloodcurdling scream ripped through the theater.

Roy instinctively wheeled toward the door.

A second scream followed, even louder than the first. Before it subsided, Roy was already on a dead run.

He threw open the center-row doors. Down the aisle, he spotted the Lone Ranger and Tonto standing in the seats. The Lone Ranger was bent over, seemingly comforting someone. Roy couldn't tell if it was a man or a woman.

Roy rushed down the aisle, his pulse pounding. As he drew closer, he saw it was an older woman.

He placed a hand on the Lone Ranger's shoulder.

The Lone Ranger straightened, stepped into the aisle, and whispered, "What are you going to do?"

Roy whispered back, "Can we get the body out of here?"

"You mean out of the theater?"

"Yeah."

"You mean actually unchain the doors and let someone come in to get it? Not on your life." The Lone Ranger's voice was flat, emotionless. "This doesn't change anything. It's unfortunate, but that's the way it goes."

He glanced down at the body. "He's dead. I don't think it makes much difference to him."

Roy swallowed. "Do you know what he died from?"

The Lone Ranger shook his head. "I hope to hell it wasn't a heart attack. If it were, we could be in big trouble. You know damned well that if he died of a heart attack, we could be charged with murder."

"Yeah," Roy murmured. "But wouldn't it be hard to prove it was because of us?"

"Let's not worry about that now," the Lone Ranger said. "Help Tonto move the body to the men's room. I'll deal with the old ladies."

Roy nodded and worked his way into the row of seats.

Tonto motioned for the two elderly women to step into the aisle. Then he and Roy half-dragged, half-carried the body up the aisle.

The audience members who could see what was happening remained silent, too terrified to react. For all they knew, the man had been some kind of threat—someone who had been forcibly subdued.

Roy didn't look at their faces.

Roy and Tonto carried the body into the men's room, maneuvering it into a cubicle. They sat it down on the closed toilet seat. Only then did they take a good look.

"He's awfully young," Roy muttered. "No doubt about it—heart attack."

He rolled up first the right sleeve, then the left. He recoiled in disgust. "Christ. He's got more tracks than the railroad."

Tonto grimaced.

"No one needs an autopsy to figure out what happened," Roy said.

He adjusted the body to keep it from sliding off the toilet. "I'm locking the door from the inside," he added, climbing over the stall.

Tonto nodded, waiting for him to land. As they walked out of the men's room, Tonto glanced toward the theater doors. "Hope the old ladies are all right."

"I'll check on the employees," Roy said.

Tonto nodded, and they split up. Inside the theater, the Lone Ranger had calmed the two elderly women. Now, he was striding toward the stage when his walkie-talkie crackled.

"T to L.R.," came Tonto's voice.

The masked man stopped at the bottom of the stage steps. "L.R. to T. Go."

Tonto, speaking from behind the double doors, kept his voice low. "The body's tucked away in a john stall. My guess? Overdose. Tracks all over his arms."

"Good work, Kemosabe," L.R. responded. "I was sweating that one. At least that puts everyone's mind at ease."

"What's Roy doing?"

"Checking the employees."

"Good. Give him a hand, then get back to me. In the

meantime, I'll give these people a quick snow job, then we'll get back to the show."

"10-4," Tonto said.

The Lone Ranger turned down the volume on his walkie-talkie and clipped it to his belt. He climbed the stairs to the center stage, then pressed the mic button three times. Immediately, the lights behind him flickered on.

He projected his voice. "Ladies and gentlemen, please remain calm."

The crowd was restless but not panicked. The two elderly women had been the only ones to lose control. The rest had fidgeted in their seats, some murmuring, some quietly crying. A few teetered on the edge of hysteria, but neighbors kept them in check.

"Please, I need your attention." The masked man held up both hands.

The murmuring died down.

"For those of you unaware, something happened a few minutes ago. A young man in the audience… is dead."

A ripple of gasps.

"I assure you, we had nothing to do with it," L.R. continued. "Two of my people checked him. He died of a drug overdose. I repeat—we had nothing to do with it. Whether it was that or something else doesn't matter. The point is, we had no hand in his death."

He let that sink in before moving on.

"From the start, we promised that no one in this theater would be hurt. And we intend to keep that promise. What happened is unfortunate, but it's over now. For your own sake, put it out of your minds."

Silence.

L.R. checked his watch.

"For whatever comfort it brings, this shouldn't take much longer. I'm expecting a call soon. When I get that call, I'll be able to tell you how soon you'll be free to go."

He scanned the room.

"In the meantime, remain calm. Keep cooperating. And just—watch the show." His voice softened. "Before you know it, you'll be home."

A pause.

"Thank you."

With that, the masked man turned, descended the stairs, and pressed the button on his walkie-talkie. Instantly, the lights dimmed, and the screen flickered to life.

The show went on.

11:38 P.M.

FINAL COUNTDOWN (TICKING CLOCK)

Police Chief Ray Boston and Mayor Lincoln Franklin sat in the back of the mayor's chauffeur-driven Continental, parked on the south side of the Mountain Theater. Less than a hundred feet away, the exit doors loomed in the darkness. The mayor turned to the Chief.

"Well?" Franklin asked.

The Chief exhaled, shaking his head. "I can only speculate. And it's a bitch, Linc. No matter how you add it up, it's a bitch." He glanced out the window. "If I had to make an educated guess—and I guess I'd have to—I'd say they're using the exit doors. The front's too exposed. There's only one emergency door in the back, and they won't funnel people through there one at a time. Too slow." He shrugged. "Has to be the exit doors."

The mayor nodded. "Which side?"

"If it were me running the show…" The Chief paused, thinking aloud. "First of all, it's a hell of a lot darker on this side. The other side faces the street, right at a busy intersection. But this side?" He gestured out the window. "Dark. Open space. No good spots for SWAT teams. If they're smart—and I think they are—they know that."

The mayor considered it. "Go on."

"There's one main exit that leads onto Topanga Canyon Boulevard. If they make it out, they can go north or south—dealer's choice. Now, here's the catch." The Chief tapped the window. "Not a single damn vehicle parked over there. If they do come out that way and somehow make it to a car, we can have Topanga locked down in seconds. They'd be boxed in. Trapped."

He leaned back. "No, Linc. It's got to be the north side. That's the only thing that makes sense. I'd bet on it."

The mayor gave a wry smile. "I hope you're a better gambler than Dangerfield. The stakes are high—and I'm not just talking about the two million dollars."

The Chief didn't need the reminder. The hell with the money, he thought. The real pot was five hundred lives. Lose that, and there was no second chance. No new deal. One hand of showdown. The winner takes all. Do or die.

He exhaled. "Tell your driver to circle around the other side. Let's get Tony in on this."

The mayor nodded but said nothing.

As the Continental rolled around the theater, Chief Boston closed his eyes, trying to unwind. He was wound too tight. Too damn tight. He didn't bother opening his eyes when he spoke.

"What about the ransom demand?"

The mayor sighed. "What about it?"

"You decided to pay?"

"That decision was made hours ago."

"So, you are paying it."

"There was never a doubt," the mayor said. "I can't play games with that many lives."

"How long to get the money together?"

"It's already done. Had it with me when I flew in from San Francisco."

The Chief nodded, opening his eyes. "Linc." He pointed at the roof of the car. "If—and I mean if—we can come up with a way to take these guys down after they free the hostages, are you in?"

The mayor studied him. "Just between you and me, Ray—once those hostages are safe, you and Tony can take your best shot. But until then? No games. No grandstanding. I run this show until every last hostage is free. After that? It's your bullfight."

The Chief took a deep breath. "Can't we block the streets? Let them think they're getting away, then close in?"

"It won't work," the mayor said. "Too many streets to cover. Too many civilians are in the way. And let's not forget—chances are, they'll take hostages with them."

The Chief cursed under his breath.

"Our best bet," the mayor continued, "is a surprise attack. Hit them hard. Fast. Before they even know what happened."

He shook his head. "Except I have no damn clue how we pull that off."

"Maybe," the Chief said slowly, "Tony'll have something. He's the best I've got. If he can't figure it out, no one can."

The mayor nodded. "Tony's a good man. Bad mouth, but good. Could've been a politician if he learned to shut up once in a while."

The Chief smirked. "Politics isn't his bag. He needs action. That's his drug."

The mayor was about to reply when he raised a hand. "Right here, Charles. Stop the car."

The vehicle slowed to a halt.

"What were you saying, Chief?"

"Forget it. Not important. Let me get Tony. We're running out of time."

Detective Tony Dangerfield, Chief Ray Boston, and Mayor Lincoln Franklin sat around a table in the makeshift command post—a dimly lit delicatessen across from the theater.

Tony pulled a crumpled piece of paper from his jacket pocket and smoothed it onto the table. Sketched across the page was a rough diagram.

"Alright," Tony muttered. "Let's figure out how the hell we end this."

Tony looked first toward Chief Boston, then to Mayor

Franklin, then at the paper.

"This is what I've come up with," he said. "On a scale of one to ten, I'd rate it zero. Frankly, it stinks. But, unfortunately," Tony said, "it's the only game in town."

"This," Tony went on, pointing to a rectangular block on the paper, "represents the theater. The lobby doors are labeled L. The glass sections of the lobby are labeled G. Everything labeled B with an arrow indicates the brick walls of the building. What we're most concerned with are labeled ED, for exit doors."

Tony took a long breath. He was weary, finding it harder and harder to concentrate. He rubbed at his eyes.

"Okay," he said, "both my ideas center around those exit doors. If I'm wrong, the whole plan isn't worth a damn. If I'm right, we may have a chance. Just a chance. I'm assuming, and don't ask me what I base my assumption on... call it whatever the hell you want. At any rate, the way I see it... my conclusion is they're going to come out these exit doors," Tony fingered the paper. "I'm assuming that when they come out, they're coming out with the ransom money. I'm also assuming that the hostages are going to be coming out either with them or before them... except for maybe one or two."

"There," Tony continued, pointing to a place above the EDs.

"This is the roof of the theater. And," he added, making little circles, "that's where I'll station my SWAT teams." Tony penciled in ST.

"I'm assuming that those SWAT teams are going to prove useless. If those guys do what I expect them to do, and that has everybody exit at just about the same time, I doubt our SWAT teams will be able to get off a shot. I don't care how good they are, and they're damned good. They'd be taking one hell of a risk shooting into the crowd that'll be spilling out of the theater."

Tony's eyes were still on the paper, and he didn't see that both the Chief and the mayor were nodding in agreement.

"The same thing goes for the SWAT teams over here," Tony said, turning to the sketch on the other side of the paper. "What this means is that all the action's going to be upfront, over here." Tony put Xs across halfway down the paper.

"Again," Tony reminded them, "don't ask me why, but it's my thinking that they're going to come out the north side of the theater. If they don't, we'll just have to play it by ear. But even if they do, we might find we've got to hold back and wait. I'm keeping in mind that your first concern is the safety of the hostages."

Tony dropped the pad on the table. "Any questions, mayor?"

"No. It's clear. So far, so good."

"Chief?"

"No questions, Tony. I'm with you."

"Okay. Now here's the tricky part," Tony drew broken lines across the bottom of the paper. "Let's say these broken lines are our police barricades with all those damned spectators behind them."

Tony drew Xs and drew a circle around them. "These are the spectators. Let me preface what comes next by saying there's a hell of a lot of risk involved. Not only to the hostages coming out, but to the spectators as well. Let me finish before you shoot me down."

"First of all, to keep the spectators behind the barricades, we're going to need an awful lot of police power." Tony drew vertical lines to represent the police and horizontal lines to represent barriers. "The one break we get," Tony said, "is that the exit doors are close together."

"Before I go any further, let me recap. Assuming we've figured right on the exit doors... on just how and when and where they're going to release the hostages... once those doors open, we've got two main concerns."

"Number one is the safety of the hostages. In other words, once they're out of the theater, it's our job to get them safely out of the area, as quickly as possible." He clicked the top of the pen.

"Objective number two: capture the kidnappers." Tony's eyes were blinking, starting to burn. He rubbed at them with the back of his left hand. He needed more black coffee. "Where was I?"

"Two concerns," the Chief prompted. "The first, the safe release of the hostages, then, nailing the kidnappers."

"Right. Okay. This is the part that's sticky. I'm going to need

18 to 25 buses...."

"You did say buses," the mayor asked quizzically.

"Yeah, buses," Tony replied sarcastically, not looking at the mayor. "You know, those things people keep paying more and more money to ride on." Tony did some more artwork. "My idea is to position these buses away from the immediate view of anybody exiting those doors. And position them in a triangular courtyard formation."

Tony drew a representation of his verbalization. "These tiny squares represent the buses. You can see, as I've drawn them, they form a tightly cordoned area. When the kidnappers open those exit doors to let the hostages out, they won't see the buses. They'll be right smack in the middle of them, and too far away from the exit doors to duck back into the theater."

"Of course, they'll soon see the buses on the front line."

Tony pointed to the squares. "But until they're quite a bit away from the doors, they won't see the buses on both sides of the triangle. They won't be aware of the courtyard trap until it's too late. As I said before, it's dangerous. We can't be sure how they're going to react once they realize they're walking into a trap."

"At this point, we'll have several options. My first idea is to have the bus doors open. We'd have cops with bullhorns urging the hostages to board the buses. Of course, my STOP Squad will be positioned under several of the buses. They'll be hidden under the buses. They won't be spotted in the darkness until the very last minute. If they can pick out any of the perpetrators, they may be able to take a couple out."

"My second thought is this: In the event that they let all the hostages out at one time, there will be chaos. In the middle of the confusion of the hostages coming out all at one time, my STOP team can get out from under the buses and mingle with the crowd. Hopefully, they'll be able to pick out the kidnappers. My third thought," Tony continued, "would be a sort of combination of both. Many of the hostages probably will head for the buses. Some of the kidnappers might be among them. So, we'll have members of the SWAT team inside the buses too."

Tony had good peripheral vision, and out of the corner of his eye, he caught the mayor shaking his head. He turned toward the black man. "I never said I liked it," Tony said defensively.

"I didn't say a word," the mayor replied, just as defensively.

"You didn't have to," Tony said sarcastically. "Like I said before, it's the only game in town."

"Let's get a pot of coffee over here," the mayor said, rubbing the back of his neck. "I want to take a closer look at these diagrams." He pulled the paper across the table.

The Chief slid out of his seat. He walked to the counter for the coffee.

Mayor Franklin was deep in Tony's diagram. Tony sat quietly, sucking the end of a ballpoint pen.

11:40 P.M.

TENSION PEAKS (CHIEF'S DILEMMA)

The tension in the Mountain Theater was getting to the audience. Several hundred people were finding it impossible to sit still. They were squirming. They were anxiously anticipating what they hoped would take place in half an hour. In approximately 30 minutes, barely enough time to show the average TV flick, the majority of the people in the theater were going to go through a lifetime of horror. They would never forget what was going to happen.

Julie didn't realize that, as her fears got worse, she had been squeezing Bryan's hand more and more tightly. The heavily initialed ring on his finger had bitten him through his skin. His pinkie was bleeding. Bryan wasn't aware of the pain or the blood. He was lost in his own fears.

In the darkness, Don Pearson was barely able to make out the hands on his watch. The show was due to let out in 25 minutes. He looked over at his kids, his wife, and his neighbor's kids. His hand rested on his wife's knee.

Don was a man of action, but not impetuous. Don knew there was nothing he could do but sit and wait, along with 500 other people. These last 25 minutes would be an eternity. His eyes were fixed on the big screen. There was a sound and a picture. Neither registered in his mind.

Don Pearson had a wife and seven kids to protect, and by God, somehow he was going to do that! He had to figure the cops would come through with the money. No way could they jeopardize the lives of the people in the theater. He could see the possibility of the police taking risks with maybe a hostage or two, or even a few, but there had to be hundreds of people in this theater—men, women, and children. The police wouldn't dare play games with the lives of so many people.

But what if they dared? What if they were taking all this time to come up with a plan of attack, and not the money? And if they attacked, the audience would be caught in the middle. What then? Don shut his eyes tightly, trying to blot out the horrible possibilities. He didn't want to know the answer to that question. But deep inside his gut, he already knew the answer.

Shutting his eyes made no difference. He still saw pictures. But not on the screen. Don stole a glance at his watch. Only two minutes had passed. He looked at the kids. They seemed to be taking things in stride. Apparently, they didn't quite understand what was happening. They were engrossed in the picture on the screen.

Don reached for June's hand. A normally nervous woman, her hands were often sweating. Now her hands were clammy. Don knew June's body reacted that way only when her anxiety began approaching hysteria.

June looked at Don. She tried unsuccessfully to force a smile. Don squeezed her hand reassuringly. Other people in the theater were starting to squirm. Don could hear the squeaking and squealing of some of the rusty seats. He could hear the sound of the wooden seat backs. He could hear Italian heels clicking against the cement floor as feet tapped impatiently, nervously. He could hear the sounds of nylon rubbing together as legs crossed and uncrossed. Don could smell the odor of fear hanging in the air.

Through all this noise, through all this chaos, through all this excitement, Danny Knight slept. He was in a world of his own. He was feeling comfortable. And Danny wasn't even aware of his feelings.

Danny's god had finally given Danny what Danny had sought. Danny had finally found the peace and serenity he had searched for so long. Danny had finally found total happiness. He was at peace with the world.

John Ruffington crossed and then uncrossed his long legs. Unconsciously, his right hand felt for his weapon. He felt the cold steel of the .357 Magnum. He fingered the grip tenderly as if he were kneading the flesh of his girlfriend's breast. Out of the corner of his eye, he kept watching the aisle door. He was waiting for the door to open. Waiting for the man who had gone to the men's room to return. Waiting to see the man dressed in Roy Rogers' outfit. John was waiting for him because he wanted to ask permission to go to the men's room. Huffington felt that he was back in a classroom. Under different circumstances, the situation could be comical. Here he was, waiting to raise his hand, waiting to ask permission of his teacher to leave the room.

Like a student set to pull a prank on his teacher, John was also waiting for his chance. As soon as that man got back from the john, as soon as Roy Rogers walked back through those double doors, John was going to put his plan into action.

It was very simple. In his mind, John ran through the plan for the fourth time. First, John told himself, he needed to get Roy's attention. Then he would ask permission to go to the head. Roy, or one of these other kidnappers, would undoubtedly escort him. They wouldn't let John go alone, that was for sure.

When he got into the john, he'd go into one of the stalls. He'd lock the door. He was sure they couldn't object to his locking the door. Hell, there was no place to go. He wasn't about to dive down the toilet.

Inside the cubicle, he'd immediately crawl into the next stall. When he'd come out, there would be two things going for him. The man was going to be caught off guard, figuring John to be in the other stall. But the bigger factor in John's favor was that the man didn't know John had a .357. After he took the man and disarmed him, he exchanged clothing. From that point, John would have to play it by ear.

John went back over his plan, searching for flaws. He couldn't find any. He liked it. It had to come off without a hitch. There were a lot of lives depending on him. He'd be the hero of the day. The man of the hour. They'd honor him at the police station. They'd probably even put a plaque with his picture on it up on the station wall. He'd be the center of attention. Be in all the newspapers and on TV. He'd certainly get a promotion. It couldn't miss. It had to work.

With his right hand, John rubbed harder at the gun grips. With his left hand, he patted his girlfriend's thigh reassuringly. At the same time, he kept his eyes on the door. It wouldn't be long now. The man dressed in the Jesse James outfit looked at the short, fat, balding projectionist. He looked at his watch and shrugged. Jesse James was bored.

"How long before that movie ends?" Jesse asked.

"About another 22 minutes," the man said in a husky voice. For the last hour, Jesse had been growing impatient. He didn't like being cooped up in such a small room. It was hot, it was sticky, and it was damp. The fact that the projectionist smoked and Jesse didn't made matters worse.

The least they could have done was give this job to somebody else. Why couldn't they have let him be downstairs, parading around in the big theater? At least he'd be able to walk around; he wouldn't be cramped. Well, he thought, less than half an hour and it would all be over. They'd all have their share of the loot. His life would be completely different.

No more having to live on a budget. No more having to cut corners, no more having to scrimp on this and save on that, no more having to do without. The next time he saw a suit he liked, or a sports jacket he liked, or a pair of slacks he felt like buying—even if he didn't need it—he'd be able to afford it.

On the slightest whim, he'd go here or there, or anywhere. Of course, he couldn't live outrageously; that would attract too much attention. Somebody might get nosy or curious. But he sure as hell would live a lot better.

The first thing he was going to do—and that wouldn't be living outrageously—was buy that outboard. The canopied job. The ski boat. Christ, he would take the kids waterskiing on weekends.

On his days off, he would take himself fishing. Maybe he could even get the wife to go along. She wasn't crazy about the water, but maybe he would teach her to waterski. Maybe they'd be a family again. Financial security relieves a lot of pressure. But first would come the boat.

Jesse glanced quickly at the projectionist. The man was sitting down, smoking another cigarette. Jesse hadn't even needed the gun. The projectionist hadn't given him a bit of trouble.

Everything was going off without a hitch. The only complaint he had was being cooped up in this cramped, smoke-filled room... but what the hell, for $285,000, he could put up with that for a few hours. It wasn't every day somebody got paid $285,000 to watch a Halloween Horror Show.

11:50 P.M.

ONE LAST TRY (DANGERFIELD'S PLEA)

The man in the Maverick costume leaned back against the doors that separated the theater from the lobby. His eyes were alert. They danced from one row of seats to another. He was watching for anything or anybody that moved wrong, that might be amiss. Things were going smoothly, he thought, too smoothly. Up to this point, everything had gone off without a hitch. He'd been confident the plan was good. But it was going even better than he had anticipated.

Maverick gripped the machine gun tightly. His eyes kept watch for anyone who might make a false move. Nobody dared. Maverick relaxed, just a bit.

Tomorrow, he thought, when he woke up, he'd be $285,000 richer. $285,000 tax-free dollars! He wondered what he'd do first with his share of the two million dollars.

11:57 P.M.

THE CLOCK TICKS (SECONDS REMAIN)

At the front of the center aisle, Wild Bill Hickok turned. Once again, he started up the aisle. With each step, he looked first to his left, then to his right.

Everything was letter-perfect; it was going off letter-perfect. He never would have dreamed it would be this easy. People on either side of the aisle weren't even bothering to look at him. Even though he was sure they weren't watching the picture, their eyes were focused on the screen. They were afraid to move, afraid to even look sideways.

He fingered the trigger of the machine gun. They were afraid of that little baby. Maverick laughed. He never would have believed it could be this easy to earn $285,000.

11:59 P.M.

TOO LATE? (DO OR DIE)

Tonto sat crouched on the soundstage step. The machine gun was cradled across his legs. His keen eyes searched the audience... particularly near the right-hand section, which was his assignment. Everything was cool. None of these turkeys, he thought to himself, had the guts to play games.

Hell, they were probably just as eager to get this thing over with as he was. Less than 20 minutes, he guessed, and they'd have their money. Then the hostages would be freed. It would be that simple.

Tonto chuckled to himself and patted the machine gun. He was about to earn himself $285,000 by merely playing "Tonto" for a few hours. What irony! All these years, he'd busted his ass to earn less than a measly living, and even then, Uncle Sam took a big chunk... for what? Not when it was this easy to make big money, to make a killing, to make that one big haul. And they had practically done it.

In less than half an hour, the mission would be completed. They would have done it. They'd have gotten away with it. The rip-off of the century.

12:01 P.M.

FALLOUT BEGINS (GUNFIRE)

The Lone Ranger leaned against the exit doors on the far side of the theater. He tested the heavy steel chains and the padlock. Everything was secure. He walked slowly up to the second set of doors. In the dim light, he felt for the heavy chain, then the lock. They, too, were secure.

He leaned against the door and looked at the hundreds of people in the theater. What a cinch! Like taking candy from a baby. Unreal! All these people were like little lost sheep. He really hadn't thought it would be this easy to terrify so many people. But they'd done it, thanks to the machine gun dangling at his side.

L.R. had insisted from the beginning that ordinary handguns or rifles, even, wouldn't have done it. Only firepower promising instant mass slaughter would be sure to strike terror in the hearts of a mass audience. Lovingly, he stroked the baby at his side. The Lone Ranger snickered contemptuously.

Just a matter of minutes, L.R. thought. 20—maybe 25 minutes at the most—and they'd each be $285,000 richer. All because they'd had the guts, the nerve, the audacity to try the seemingly impossible.

What the hell, L.R. thought, like the commercial says—YOLO; you only live once. Grab for all the gusto. And they had grabbed for it. They had taken a shot at the whole enchilada, and it was about to become theirs. The whole plan had gone smoothly. It was a pitcher's dream. The perfect game. They were winners from wire to wire—only this race paid long odds; very, very long odds. 285,000 to 1 odds.

The Lone Ranger saw green as he walked up the aisle.

12:07 P.M.

AFTERMATH (CHAOS UNFOLDS)

At the exact moment, the Lone Ranger started walking up the aisle, Roy Rogers and the man he had escorted to the john stepped out of the lavatory. Slowly, they walked toward his seat.

Roy's mind was savoring $2,000,000. The man in front of him was thinking about death. And behind those heavy double doors, John Ruffington's hand sweated in nervous anticipation. John was waiting for his chance. His chance to save the lives of 500 people. His chance to return to the County of Los Angeles, their investment in John Ruffington.

11:41 P.M.

UNRAVELLING (REWIND MOMENT)

"I don't like it," the mayor said emphatically. "There's got to be a better way."

"Well, if there is," Tony said simply, "let's hear it."

The mayor ran his finger around the rim of his coffee cup. "Okay," he said, nodding his head and taking a closer look at the diagram. "... Let's say we go with this part here..." The mayor pointed to the buses. "Assuming," the mayor continued, "that we all agree we want to use the buses. It seems to me that the situation we'll end up with will be the same as we've got on our hands now."

"Supposing," the mayor said, closing his eyes and trying to picture what Tony had in mind. "Supposing they get their ransom and then release the hostages. They all come streaming out of the theater into the parking lot. A parking lot with a concentration of empty buses... I would think," the mayor continued, "that most of the people are going to jump on the buses."

Tony was nodding.

"Certainly," the mayor said, and it came out half-question, half-statement. "Certainly, some of the kidnappers are going to end up on the buses with hostages...."

"I would imagine so," Tony said, matter-of-factly.

"Alright," the mayor said, like a trial lawyer making his

summation. "Then we're right back where we started."

Tony fingered a fresh Havana cigar. "Not really. With 18 to 25 buses out there," Tony continued. "Chances are you're going to end up with somewhere between 25 and 30 people on a bus. Obviously, there aren't that many kidnappers. So you aren't going to have a kidnapper on each bus. The final part of that plan," Tony finished, "is to have three policemen on each bus. One will be a member of the SWAT team; one a trained sharpshooter; and the man in the driver's seat will be a uniformed policeman."

"In other words, let me give it to you in a nutshell. Actually, you're going to have an almost identical situation, but on a smaller scale. I guess you could call it the principle of divide and conquer. You've got fewer people in a concentrated area, which should reduce the chance of shooting. We'll have the kidnappers outnumbered, and we'll have the element of surprise working for us."

Tony pointed his cigar in the mayor's direction. "That's the best I can do."

The mayor put his head back and stared at the ceiling. For a long 30 seconds, there was a deafening silence.

The Chief broke the silence. "Your STOP squad, Tony, where are they going to be deployed?"

"I told you before, they'll be under the buses. When the exit doors are open, and the hostages start coming out, they'll crawl out from under the buses and mingle with the hostages and the kidnappers. They'll be trying to ferret out the kidnappers. Of course, the odds of them doing this aren't fantastic, but at least they'll be in a position to move in any direction."

"Jesus," the Chief whistled. "I think the mayor's right, Tony. We'd be taking one hell of a risk."

"I said it before, boss. It's the only game in town."

"Not quite. There is one other game."

"What's that?" Tony asked.

"Don't hassle them, period. Give them the money. Give them enough slack to do what they want."

"And play catch-up later?" Tony asked.

"And play catch-up later," the Chief responded.

"No," Tony said. "I can't buy that. I can see giving them room. I can see giving them plenty of room. But I can't see giving them carte blanche. It won't work, boss."

Tony's face went sour. "That's one hell of an open invitation, boss. Not even putting up token resistance?"

"I can see the headlines in tomorrow's paper," Tony's finger traced a headline in the air. "Kidnappers were given $2,000,000 and police protection. Authorities aid and abet fugitives. Sound good?" Tony asked, looking first at the Chief, then at the mayor. "Play it your way, that's what you're going to see tomorrow. Mark my words. I'm not trying to tell you that my way's the right way. It may not work. It may be dangerous as hell and G.D. chancy as hell. But it sure beats a free trip past go. Besides," Tony added, saving the best for last. "Your way could cost you a lot of votes."

"You're also forgetting," Tony continued, "they have automatic weapons. The minute they step outside the theater with those automatic weapons, my men take aim from fifteen different directions. I've got sharpshooters out there. Men trained with weapons. If the proximity wasn't as close as it is, maybe there'd be a chance they'd mess up. But that's literally like shooting ducks in a pond. I got my men in the middle of that pond. These clowns are out there with their weapons exposed. My men are going to castrate them."

"Are you going to have your men fire into the middle of that crowd?" the mayor interjected.

Tony slapped an open hand on the table. It wasn't an act of defiance; it was an attention-getting device. "I've got some of my men, Mr. Mayor, positioned on the roof of that theater. They're looking down at these men. First of all, they're trained SWAT teams. They're trained to handle crises like this. They're not going to fire if there's any danger to innocent people.

"But believe me, if they get a chance, they'll be ready. And when they have that chance, they're not going to blow it. It's going to be over like this." Tony snapped his fingers. "They're up high, Mr. Mayor." Tony pointed his thumb toward the sky. "They're up on the damned roof, looking down. Can you picture that? .....Sir."

The mayor swallowed hard. The words that followed took Tony by surprise.

"Okay, Tony. I'll buy it. But only on one condition."

"Shoot."

"Your men," the mayor warned, slowly, deliberately, "are to be given strict instructions that under no circumstances are they to fire until they are positive they have a clear field of vision. If there is any risk whatever to a bystander, a hostage, or anyone but a perpetrator, they are to hold their fire. Is that fair enough?"

"Fair enough."

"But those damned buses," the mayor seemed to be talking to himself. "I still don't like that."

"If either one of you can come up with a better plan, I'll be glad to try it for size. Meanwhile," Tony looked at his watch, "we're running out of time."

"How long do we have?" the Chief asked.

"20 minutes," Tony said. "Give or take a couple of minutes."

"We can buy time," the mayor said. "All I have to do is call and tell them we're having trouble getting the money. They're probably expecting that anyway."

"Why get them more on edge?" Tony offered. "If they think they've got all the cards stacked in their favor, maybe they'll get careless and make the one mistake we're waiting for."

"If we start playing games, they're going to get suspicious. If they get suspicious, they'll get more cautious. If it's going to lean, let's have it lean our way. Let them be cocky. Then, boom! One mistake, and we close the net."

"I can't argue with that," the Chief nodded, looking to the mayor for agreement.

"I'm with you. Let's not get them hinky. But I'm going on record as being against the buses."

"You can go on record any way you want, Mr. Mayor," Tony said. "But we're running out of time. If we can't come up with a better plan, we'll have to go with it."

"Okay," the mayor said. Then, pointing his finger at Tony, he added, "But all men inside those buses are to be instructed that under no circumstances are they to get trigger-happy. They don't fire until you personally give the order."

"My men," Tony said defiantly, "are not trigger-happy. They're hand-picked experts."

The mayor closed his eyes as if that would make Tony disappear. Tony stopped abruptly; the mayor cut in.

"They're human, Tony. They're not machines. Human beings make mistakes. If you're looking to cut down on the odds, I'm looking to cut down on the margin of error. Understand?"

Tony had no argument. The mayor's point was valid and well-taken. "You're right. A hundred percent. My men will be given those precise instructions."

"Let me know, mayor, 10 minutes before you're ready to make the payoff. I'll have my men briefed and ready."

"Okay. I think everything's as set as we're going to get it," the Chief concluded. Tony agreed.

The mayor looked to the Chief. "I've got no questions." Tony looked first at the Chief, then at the mayor. "I have a question. How soon before you're ready to go ahead with the payoff?"

"That's up to you. I'm willing to call the theater and buy time. You're the one who doesn't want to get them on edge."

"I agree with Tony," the Chief added quickly.

"Okay," the mayor said easily. "Then we agree. We go ahead with the payoff. On time."

"If you can have the money ready by then," Tony said, "all I need time for is to brief my men. Then I'm free to make the delivery."

The mayor tapped the edge of his saucer. He took a deep breath. "The money, Tony, is ready when you are. It's here. The whole two million dollars."

12:08 P.M.

BACKLASH (GUNMEN REACT)

John Ruffington sat at the edge of his seat... anxious, apprehensive, unsure of himself, scared. John's mind had written a script. Now his body had to play the part. If the scene went well, he would win the Oscar. If he so much as blew a line, the curtain could come down, not only on him but on his entire audience, forever.

Suddenly, the double doors opened. John watched the first man walking down the aisle, Roy Rogers behind him.

John mumbled encouragement to himself, trying to keep calm, as the men approached. He closed his eyes tightly for a split second, then waited for his cue.

As the men were about to come abreast of his row, John turned toward the aisle, and raising his hand high, he asked, "May I go to the john?"

Roy Rogers turned toward the voice, annoyance on his face. "Can't it wait a while?" he asked John, looking from his watch to Ruffington.

John shook his head. "I've been waiting," John said. "I can't wait anymore. I gotta go." As foolish as John Ruffington felt, he was playing his role well.

John now sat silently, crossing and uncrossing his legs. Then he put his hand on his abdomen.

Roy Rogers made sure his charge got back to his seat. Roy looked at Huffington again. "If you got to go," the costumed cowboy sighed, "I guess you got to go. Come on," he said, motioning for John to get up.

Huffington squeezed his girlfriend's hand as he stood up.

He winked, but in the dimness, he was sure she didn't notice.

He had to step past three people to get to the aisle. He did so, slowly, gingerly. With his left hand, he held close the bottom of his sports jacket.

The .357 Magnum is a big weapon. If the jacket snagged on a seat back or brushed against someone's hand or leg, it could expose the gun. So his steps were short, smooth, and certain as he stepped sideways past one person, then another, and then past the last hazard and into the aisle.

The man in the Roy Rogers costume motioned for John to walk in front of him, then followed cautiously about three feet behind John.

Huffington walked slowly, his hands in plain sight at his side. He didn't want to give the man behind him reason for suspicion.

Above the sounds from the screen, and in spite of the carpeted aisle, John could hear Roy's faint footsteps. John could hear his own heartbeat.

John looked at the double doors. They were 20 feet away. He reminded himself to move slowly, casually. When John reached for the door, he was going to do so very slowly, keeping both hands in plain sight.

Hopefully, he'd also be able to add the right touch of nervousness to his role. If the man behind him, the man in the cowboy costume, noticed that John was nervous, that would add to John's performance. His captor would pay him less attention: he would be off guard.

Before reaching for the door, John turned, anxiously looking back over his shoulder. The brim of the cowboy's hat was no more than six inches away.

"Are you waiting for me to open the door?" Roy asked impatiently. "You're the one who's got to go."

Slowly, John eased the door open. Then, uncertain, he hesitated, looking back at the cowboy. Should he hold the door open for Roy? But his question was answered as the cowboy reached for the door. Again, impatiently, he motioned to John to keep walking.

John turned to his left and walked through the lobby. His strides were a little longer, a little faster, to match the urgency of his need to relieve himself.

As John neared the "Men's Room" sign, his arms moved like slow pendulums at his sides. The left arm deliberately brushed against his jacket, reassuring John that his prop was in waiting.

John ran his tongue over his lips. He was beginning to feel like a victim. Not a cop. The oppressed. Not the aggressor. His hands were clammy. His knees felt weak as he reached for the door marked "Men's Room."

Huffington didn't look back as he stepped onto the tiled floor. His left arm brushed against his side as he walked across the room to the cubicle. He listened for the continuing rhythmic clicking of heels. As he reached the stall door, he stopped and listened, but the heels had stopped clicking. The submachine-carrying Western bandit was chaperoning him from a leaning position against the far wall. John took a deep breath. He hoped he would have many more breaths.

John stood in front of the cubicle. He pushed the gray door. It opened easily. Glancing over his shoulder, John stepped inside the stall. His costumed captor leaned against the sink, eyeing John cautiously. John closed the cubicle door. After his trained eye quickly surveyed the bathroom.

John was playing a real-life and death game. His life, and probably the lives of a few hundred hostages, hung in the balance.

John Huffington locked the cubicle door. Fully clothed, he sat on the toilet. It took him less than ten seconds to slide out of his shoes. Another 20 seconds, and he had slid silently into the adjoining cubicle. It had taken John Ruffington less than a minute to make the switch.

John had left his shoes positioned in the empty stall. If a cowboy should happen to look under the cubicle, he'd see shoes. That would keep him happy for the brief minute more that John would need. At least John hoped it would.

John realized the advantage he held over the cowboy who held him at bay. The advantage, razor-thin as it was, might turn out to be the edge John needed. John patted the gun reassuringly. He kept his eyes glued to the stall door. He held his breath and began easing himself down onto the toilet seat. His ears strained for any sound that might betray him.

If the cowboy so much as started to walk around on the tiled floor, John would be alerted by the first click of a heel.

He started to squat. No sound. He was sure his guard suspected nothing. Everything was going precisely as planned, John reassured himself. John was giving the perfect performance. If he could keep it up, he'd have won his first battle and might well be on his way to winning the war.

Without taking his eyes off the stall door, JR let his backside ease down toward the toilet seat. As his balance shifted to the lower portion of his back, John reached across his body with his right hand, feeling for his .357 magnum on his hip.

In one well-practiced motion, John had the gun out. He flipped the barrel open, checking the load. John's eyes found six bullets in as many chambers. At this point, John's ass should have made contact with the toilet seat. But suddenly, John's stomach went queasy. There was a very sharp pain in the pit of his stomach; a sweeping nausea in his gut.

John leaped to his feet, whirling around. He tried to tighten his grip on the .357. It was too late. The gun slipped from John's hand and crashed to the marble floor, sliding out of the stall, away from John's desperate hands.

John Ruffington stood stone still, not believing what he was seeing. A fully clothed young man sat still and erect on the throne. John's training wasn't needed to tell him that the young man was either out cold or dead.

But John's training did tell him that the latter was probably true. He tried to clear his head and calm himself. He tried to tell himself that somehow this thing would still work.

John was vaguely aware of something that sounded like clothes rustling. But the sound seemed far off. He was more acutely aware of a dull pressure in the small of his back. As he half-turned, a sixth sense told John that he and the young man on the throne were not alone in the stall. And he was aware that he'd completely fucked up. And he was more aware of the fact that he was in grave danger.

So, doing the only thing that made sense, Officer John Ruffington turned. He faced squarely the cowboy with the machine gun. John Huffington uttered clearly and succinctly the first words that entered his mind: "Oh shit!"

There was a faint smile on Roy Rogers' face. But that smile did little to reassure Officer John Huffington. The machine gun leveled at his midsection did even less. This thought, John, is curtain time.

John watched as Roy sized him up. John waited. He wanted something to happen. The machine gun John so desperately wanted to clutch in his hands was in the hands of the enemy. John was where he had started. Only worse now. He had been caught at his own game. The enemy reached back, unsnapping the lock. He stepped forward, the muzzle pressed into John's belly, forcing John backward.

Roy opened the door of the stall. He backed out, holding the door so John could follow. "Hands on the sink, asshole," Roy said, motioning with the machine gun. "Your weight on the palms of your hands, wise guy. One move and you'll never see your shoes again." Roy patted the machine gun. John did as he was ordered.

John once more felt weak in the knees. But far worse was his humiliation, his fear. John was used to being the aggressor. He was the one to shake down a prisoner. He was the one to make the hard-assed, smart-assed cracks. Now the roles were reversed. John cursed himself.

John swerved slightly to the left. Out of the corner of his eye, he could see Roy kneeling, scooping up the .357. "Nice," Roy said, examining the grips. "Bet one of these babies does a hell of a lot of damage."

Not half the damage, John worried, that that machine gun could do.

"Now what the hell would somebody like you," Roy said aloud, "be doing with something like this?"

Oh shit, John thought. Now all the cowboy had to do was get hinky enough to frisk him and pull his I.D. John realized he wasn't out of the woods yet. He could still end up sitting on the throne next to the dead kid. This whole thing was so stupid, so absurd. It was a bad dream, except this time, John might not wake up.

John thought it was worse than a B-movie. If he saw something like this Late Show, he'd turn it off and go to sleep.

"Cop or crook?" Roy asked suddenly, breaking the silence. "Which?"

John shifted his weight to the balls of his feet. Something told him no matter what he said, it was going to be wrong. Odds are, the clown was going to search him anyway.

Suddenly, John stood erect. He did a quick about-face. He looked straight at Roy, feet from him. The machine gun extended to John's stomach.

"I'm a cop," John said. "Actually, I'm a rookie with West Valley." John Ruffington didn't blink. He didn't move. He stared directly into the eyes of the enemy. John waited for the rat-a-tat-tat of the machine gun. Or did they say you were dead before you heard the noise?

Nothing happened. Roy apparently respected John's defiance.

For some reason, John Ruffington's mind flashed, for a fleeting second, to Snoopy and the Red Baron at Christmas. "Any more heat, cop?" Roy asked softly.

John looked down at the floor. He shook his head. "No."

"Not even handcuffs?"

"No. I left them home," John said honestly. Roy nodded.

"Can I take you at your word?"

John nodded.

"You don't happen to have any more ammunition on you?" Roy asked.

John shook his head. He watched Roy empty the magnum.

"You'll find this hard to believe," the masked man said, "but

I've always respected cops. If I were in your shoes, I'd feel castrated if somebody took my gun."

The masked man stepped forward and handed John back the magnum. "Put it away," Roy said gently. "I'll give you credit," Roy said, "for what you tried. But believe me, this is a war you can't win. You can't go up against all the firepower we've got. Your smartest move would be to play it cool. You're just another victim. We'll get what we came for, and that'll be it. We're not going to hurt anybody. Not if you don't give us the reason.

"What happened to the kid?" Roy looked in the direction of the stall.

"It wasn't any of our doing. Lousy timing. I'd guess a drug overdose. But a doctor I'm not," Roy said, trying to impress John with his sincerity.

"Use your head," Roy said. "Think about the other 500 people. They'd like to get home to their families and their kids. If you try to fuck things up, you can only cause them trouble. Take my word for it. Let it slide."

Roy looked at his watch. "The whole thing can be history in a matter of minutes. Why don't we just go back out and make it like nothing happened? Nobody has to know. When the final tape is tallied, is it going to really matter?"

A voice that wasn't John's, that wasn't Roy's, told Huffington that he'd just been granted amnesty. It also told Huffington that there was more to this than met the eye.

Without another word, Ruffington walked to the john door. Without listening, he knew those heels were clicking a few feet behind. Without turning to look, John knew that the machine gun was at ease at Roy's side. Without arguing with himself, JR conceded that as far as he was concerned, the war was over. He had lost.

12:10 A.M.

BLOOD AND SMOKE (FIREFIGHT)

Outside the theater, the crowd had swelled. Reinforcements were called in from the Van Nuys and North Hollywood Divisions. Some of the spectators had become so unruly that several dozen had been carted away and threatened with arrest or actually booked for disorderly conduct. The crowd seemed to be divided into three categories: those who were genuinely concerned, those who were looking to see blood spilled, and those who were bored and were out to kill time.

Christ! The people were abandoning their cars in the middle of Topanga Canyon Boulevard. There wasn't even enough police power to cite all the vehicles. Traffic cops were being used for crowd control. The crowd belonged at home, minding their own business, leaving the police free to do police work.

The barricades that had been placed around the expansive perimeter of the theater had been threatened by the curious onlookers.

Dozens of uniformed policemen had to be taken away from other posts to man barricades and keep back the swelling crowds of people trying to force their way beyond the wooden structures. There was an obvious shortage of manpower. This meant that police had to be borrowed from other divisions, and that meant that those divisions were going to be left shorthanded. Off-duty police officers were being called back to work on emergency status.

An entire nation was watching what was going on in this Woodland Hills city. The situation was so damned delicate, so different from anything that had ever happened before, that everyone was uncertain of the next move. The only thing anyone knew for a fact was that 500 lives were at stake, and time was growing short—very short.

12:18 A.M.

THE DEAL BREAKS (ESCAPE BEGINS)

Tony Dangerfield was waiting for the $2,000,000 that he was about to carry inside the theater. He was thinking of the 500 terrified people inside that theater who were waiting on that money, waiting in exchange for their lives.

Mayor Lincoln Franklin's Continental pulled up. The mayor jumped out and hurried over to Tony, hand extended toward him. Hesitantly, Tony reached for the black hand. Reluctantly, he shook hands with LAF.

"Good luck!" the mayor said. "Remember: No games. No grandstanding."

Tony Dangerfield looked into the dark eyes. "Don't worry," he said. "There are a lot of votes in there. I'll protect them."

The mayor's hand fell away limply. Without a word, the mayor turned from Tony Dangerfield, bowed his head, and prayed. Tony walked toward the police van, parked 20 yards from the barricades. Inside the doors of the van, guarded by eight uniformed cops, was the ransom money.

There, thought Dangerfield, as he walked to the police van, were get-out-of-jail-free cards for 500 people. Inside that van, Tony realized, was a new lease on life. Tony nodded to half a dozen uniformed cops, then reached for the handle and $2,000,000 in cash.

12:12 A.M.

STANDOFF (SPLIT DECISION)

Inside the theater, Julie was fighting to keep control. She thought for a minute about her mother and her father, and how worried they must be. Her mother, she knew, would be going out of her mind. She always thought of the worst possibilities. Julie felt worse for her mom than she did for herself.

Her father was much more level-headed. He always tried to remain calm, at least on the outside. He might have fooled her mother, but he never fooled Julie. On the inside, Julie knew, he'd be just as worried about her, probably more. Yet he'd try his best not to show it.

Julie was perceptive enough to know that he often burned off tension by pacing up and down the living room floor. When it really got bad, he took long walks.

She wondered what he was doing tonight.

Bryan took one very, very deep breath. Then almost as slowly, he exhaled. Sitting in the theater for the last couple of hours, his mind focused on the things he had always wanted to do. He thought he was probably acting like a child because now he feared he might not get to do those things. Yet it also seemed kind of dumb to worry about all the little things in life when something like this could change everything.

Unfortunately, Bryan told himself, there was really nothing to worry about. It was stupid to worry about something you couldn't do anything about. And Bryan sure couldn't do anything about this situation.

What he could do, however, was keep himself calm. And by doing that, he'd help Julie keep calm. Maybe some of the people around him would be reassured by his attitude. Bryan made himself one promise as he squirmed in his seat, trying to dry his hands on his pants and moisten his lips with his tongue. Bryan promised himself that no matter what happened, he would protect Julie.

If somehow he had a choice, he would be it, not Julie. He'd protect Julie to the very end.

In the rear corner of the theater, where they'd decided to sit to be out of harm's way, were Nancy and her boyfriend. Nancy leaned her head back, closed her eyes, and laughed. "Out of harm's way"—the phrase stuck in her mind. It was ironic, Nancy thought. Or maybe somebody was trying to tell her something. Maybe in her own way, she was being as cruel and cold and calculating as the people who'd taken over this theater.

Maybe what she was doing to three people was not a criminal offense, but the game was just as deadly.

Maybe, Nancy told herself, keeping her eyes tightly shut, she wasn't the innocent victim she had convinced herself she was. Maybe it was time she grew up. Maybe it was time she faced the real facts of life. Maybe it was time she stood on her own two feet and faced the music she composed.

Maybe it was time to stop playing games with her marriage, to sit down and talk things out with her husband, and try to make it work. Then, and only then, would she be giving the three of them an honest shake. Then, if things didn't work, she'd be prepared for the next step.

Deep down inside, Nancy felt that her marriage could work. It was not the perfect relationship. But what is? Once they shared enough love to get married, if they were both willing to face their problems honestly and openly, the relationship had a chance.

If, after a fair trial period, it didn't work, then it could be broken off cleanly. Nancy had a neighbor who had somewhere picked up an expression that Nancy liked. It was the initials of a word. When she was uptight, her friend would remind her: How was Honesty, Open-mindedness, and Willingness.

It was for sure, Nancy scolded herself, that she hadn't been honest. All she had to do was look to her right. As for open-mindedness, well, she obviously hadn't been that either. If she had, she wouldn't have shut the door on the biggest part of their relationship. And as for the willingness, hell, for a long time now, Nancy hadn't been at all willing.

Nancy thought back to the night she'd finally accepted the reality that he'd never quit the force. She'd realized she'd always have to live with the hazards of his job. Now Nancy wondered if she'd been kidding herself. Was that the real reason?

She had married him, knowing full well that the Department would remain his career. She had loved him enough, knowing that, to marry him. Nancy sure as hell could have had her pick of guys. Some of them could have provided her with much more security, both financial and emotional, than Tony. But she had chosen him.

Maybe, if she came to grips with reality, honestly stripping away the camouflage, it became a question of attitude. Her attitude. And maybe, if she gave Tony a chance, she'd be surprised at the results.

Well, she sighed. At least she was making a decision. The ironic part of the whole thing was that if these sick, demented kidnappers saw fit to do harm to some of the people in the theater, Nancy might not have to worry about a new beginning to her marriage or anything else.

Trying not to be obvious, Don glanced at his wife. Jesus, he thought, she's beautiful. Young, vivacious, warm, tender. At the same time, it is strong and reliable. Don swallowed hard. If there were reasons for everything, why this? He leaned across the seat and kissed the top of Debbie's head. Debbie sat calmly, apparently oblivious to their predicament. Her eyes were glued to the movie screen. Don wondered if this was her way of tuning out or if she was just not aware.

He looked at the other kids. Seven-year-old Linda and eight-year-old Tracy were asleep. Tina, the oldest, was leaning against her mom's shoulder. Don wondered who was comforting whom.

Don couldn't tell whether Tina's eyes were open or shut, whether she was asleep or awake. Two of the three neighbors' kids were asleep. The third, like Debbie, seemed to be engrossed in the movie. Don guessed they were too young to understand. He looked at his watch. It was twelve minutes past midnight. They couldn't have much longer to wait. He sighed heavily. The seeming eternity would climax shortly. He only hoped it would be a non-violent climax.

June sat erect in her seat, Tina's head against her shoulder. She wanted to move the sleeping child, yet she didn't want to risk waking her. And she didn't want to put her clammy hands on her daughter.

June, who believed she always looked composed, was rapidly losing control. She was acutely aware that her dinner kept trying to come up. Her stomach was one big knot. She'd wanted to go to the ladies' room, but she was sure her legs wouldn't carry her the distance.

June was not afraid to admit it. She was terrified. Terrified, not only for herself but for her children. For Don. For the neighbor's kids. And for that matter, for everybody else in the theater. This had to be the worst experience of her life.

June wondered how Don was doing. She wanted to look over at him, but she was afraid. She was afraid that if she did, she might scream. She knew the show was coming to an end. That meant it wouldn't be long. It wouldn't be long before whatever was going to happen would happen. June shivered at the thought. She wondered if she'd get to say, "I love you,

Don," or ever again kiss the kids goodnight.

12:12 A.M.

CLOSING IN (OUTSIDE)

Tony Dangerfield slammed the door of the green police van. He turned slowly and walked back toward the entrance to the Mountain Theater. It was twelve minutes past twelve.

Just in front of Tony were four uniformed policemen. A cop stood to either side of the plastic trash container. Two other cops stood in front of the trash barrel. They led the way into the theater.

Tony looked to the rear. Behind him were two more uniformed cops. Normally, it didn't take seven cops to dispose of a trash can. This morning, it did.

Inside this particular light green plastic trash container was exactly $2,000,000 in cash. The bills were stacked in denominations of ones, fives, tens, twenties, fifties, and hundreds. They were neatly bundled in bank wrappers and piled in packets of $5,000.

Tony looked first to his left and then to his right. He watched each step taken by the uniformed policemen. Inside the refuse container were the hopes of some 500 people.

As the cops neared the theater steps, Tony's mind replayed the directions given by the mayor. Tony's instructions were clear and precise.

The kidnappers had given permission to use as many cops as necessary to carry the money to the theater stairs. At that point, the cops would turn and walk away, leaving the trash container with the $2,000,000 at the top of the stairs outside the lobby.

Tony was to remain behind, to guard the money, and to help carry the container inside the theater. Once inside the theater, the money would be checked by the kidnappers. When, and only when, they were certain that the full amount was correct, that the denominations were correct, that the money was in no way marked or otherwise tampered with, Tony Dangerfield would be given another set of instructions—a final set of instructions. When he left the theater, he would relay to his Chief and to the mayor.

This, the mayor was assured, would be the signal, providing everything was in order, to begin the freedom march for the Hostages.

As Tony was about to start on his $2,000,000 mission, the mayor firmly reminded him of the kidnapper's latest warning: "Get cute, and we'll kill a hostage." Then the mayor shook Tony's hand and wished him luck.

Six uniformed cops and a weary, solemn-looking Tony Dangerfield paused at the top of the theater steps. Inside the theater, the lobby was empty. As if on cue, the two policemen set down the trash receptacle containing the $2,000,000. Six uniformed policemen now engulfed Tony in one large circle. They turned toward him, awaiting his instructions.

Tony sighed, rubbed at the day-old growth of beard, and nodded to the men. He waved his left hand in the direction of the parking lot, indicating they could leave.

Tony Dangerfield watched as the uniformed policemen retraced their steps. Only when they had split the distance between the theater and the street did Tony turn around and look into the theater lobby.

Tony hadn't seen him. Suddenly, a man walked toward him inside the lobby. The man, dressed as Tonto, wore a black mask. Tony was expressionless as the Indian approached the lobby doors. Dangerfield watched the Injun undo the chains that secured the door. It took the Tonto-look-alike a full minute to free all the chains.

When the Indian had completed that chore, Tonto took twenty more seconds to scan the parking lot. Satisfied that there was nobody hiding in wait, Tonto took a second key from his pocket and unlocked the double doors.

Convinced now that no posse was waiting in ambush, Tonto swung open the doors and stepped out onto the landing. Quickly, he grabbed the handle of the trash receptacle, and when Tony had a grasp on his side, they walked the trash container into the theater.

They set the plastic trash can down in the lobby. Then, Tonto carefully locked and chained the doors. The Indian and the white man then carried the trash receptacle away from the lobby doors.

When they were in front of the candy counter, Tonto turned to Tony. "This way, Kimosabe," he said, without a smile, pointing to the refreshment stand. When they were out of sight of observers on the outside, they stopped, setting down the green barrel.

Tonto rubbed his right arm. Tony Dangerfield stood staring at him. "Wampum heavy," the cop said, clowning.

Tonto stopped rubbing and looked at the cop. "For that kind of wampum," the Indian said evenly, "we'd have sold you everything east of the Mississippi."

"They should have left you on the reservation," Tony reassured. "Why don't we cut the crap and get this show on the road? Let's not press our luck."

"Patience, Kimosabe," Tonto said. "Rome wasn't built in a day."

Tony Dangerfield reached for the walkie-talkie. He held the talk button down with his thumb. "Tinkers to Evers," Tony said and then waited.

Within seconds, the Chief replied. "Evers here. Go."

"Everything's under control, boss," Tony said. "I've made contact. Everything's going according to plan. They want me to watch them check out the money. I'll be pretty busy in here." Tony released the button.

"Okay," the Chief said. "Keep me posted."

"Okay," Tony replied. "I'm going to turn this thing off and concentrate on more pressing matters. 10-4?"

"That's a 10-4," his boss said.

"Clear," Tony said, releasing the button and clicking the machine off. Tony shrugged his shoulders at the Indian and sighed. "Injun know how to count wampum?" T.D. asked.

Tonto stared back at Tony. "White man know how to read numbers?"

"Touche," Tony said.

Laughing heartily, both men leaned over the green trash receptacle.

Tony counted out his share of the money, stuffing the packets into every conceivable pocket. He had deliberately worn a sports jacket with two sets of inside pockets, wide and deep. Under the sports jacket, Tony wore a loose-fitting blue vest. He stuffed packets in the vest and in his belt. More packets went into his trouser pockets. Tony hid the remaining packets in his socks, Navy fashion, and inside his high-backed boots. Tony smoothed his trouser leg over the boots.

Staring down into the trash receptacle, even after he removed his share of the loot—$285,000—the barrel was still loaded with green. He had never seen that much money. Tony kept staring in disbelief.

"Wipe your chin, White Man," Tonto interrupted.

Tony snickered, nodded, and pinched himself. But he couldn't take his eyes off the money.

"Don't get greedy, White Man. The rest of the tribe is waiting for theirs. We've got a schedule to follow," he reminded Tony, pointing to his watch. "Let's get a move on."

Tony finally tore his eyes away from the barrel. He looked at the Indian, patting his pockets. “Right,” Tony said, reaching over and slapping Tonto on the shoulder. “Let’s go,” he said, stealing a last glance at the barrel. “Walk me to the door.”

Tonto nodded. “Wampum buy plenty ponies. Maybe even a race track.”

“Fuck you,” Tony said, buttoning the front of his jacket. He checked himself out as they walked, making sure there were no bulges.

Tonto unsnapped the locks and undid the chains. He checked the parking area carefully before opening the doors. “Good luck, Kimosabe,” he said to Tony as he swung the door open wide.

Tony turned. “Don’t take any wooden nickels.” The cop stepped out into the night.

Tonto carefully rechained and relocked the doors. He walked back to the barrel of money. It took Tonto longer to count out and hide his share of the money. Underneath his costume, Tonto wore his soft clothes. Making sure his money was securely secreted was more difficult than Tonto had anticipated.

Tonto had to be certain nothing stuck out. There was no time to screw up. The war was almost over. They were about to light the peace pipe.

When Tonto had the last of his money together and when he was satisfied it was stashed, he reached for his walkie-talkie.

"T to L.R."

"L.R. to T. Go."

"You're on deck," Tonto said.

"10-4. I'm going to duck out now."

"10-4," Tonto said, turning off the machine.

As the Lone Ranger stood over the barrel, counting his share of the take, Tonto took LR's place inside the theater.

For those theatre goers who were watching the picture, they knew the movie was rapidly reaching its conclusion. The moment of truth was near; very near.

Tony Dangerfield began preparing for the release of the hostages. This was the part of the plan Tony liked the least.

He gave instructions to 30 uniformed cops before they started from the northeast corner of the theater lot. They began a slow, wide sweep of the parking area. As the cops advanced along in a tight line, onlookers were forced back toward the northwest corner of the lot.

With the practiced efficiency of the crowd-control police team, it took 18 minutes to move the crowd back to the corner. Mission accomplished, the entire northeast section of the parking area was empty of all but official personnel. Now they began moving passenger buses, driven by police personnel, into position.

Each bus contained three passengers. Each passenger wore a green police uniform, complete with a bulletproof vest. Each carried an automatic weapon. All were members of the SWAT team. The top officials stood bunched together, supervising the vehicles being positioned.

Mayor Franklin looked away. "I want to hear it again, Tony. Show me, one more time."

Ignoring the mayor, Tony yelled at the driver of one bus to keep backing up. "Don't stop until the ass end is against the building," Tony shouted. "Don't stop until you feel brick," he said emphatically.

Now he turned toward the mayor. "Okay," Tony said. "For the last time. We're assuming that they're coming out on this side. If they come out the south side, we're fucked."

"I'm assuming that most of the hostages, if they come out, will do what comes naturally and head toward the buses. As they're streaming out, my men are going to join in with them unobtrusively. I've got men all over the place," Tony said, pointing to the roof of the theater, the tops of the buses, and inside the buses. Tony then turned back to the mayor.

"I'm going to have six of my best men," Tony said, "my STOP squad, underneath those buses. They'll be in position, ready. As soon as the hostages start pouring out, those men will be right in the thick of things, taking out many of the kidnappers they can spot in the group. Each bus contains three SWAT men. Their job is twofold."

"First, they're to protect the hostages who get on the buses. Secondly, if any kidnappers go for the buses, my men will be there to nail them." Tony added hopefully: "One way or another."

"Each bus driver is an expert marksman," Tony noted, "and has an automatic weapon, a bulletproof vest, and a walkie-talkie. If anything—anything whatsoever," Tony repeated emphatically, "goes haywire, each driver has orders to move the buses immediately. I'll be out here along with you and Ray. We'll all have bullhorns."

"If the operation starts to fall apart, we'll pull back and give the kidnappers full rein. The second we even think there's a threat to life, we'll get the buses the hell out."

The mayor shook his head, but he remained silent. He had had his chance to overrule Tony earlier, in the delicatessen. He hadn't. Now it was too late. The mayor checked the time. The show would be getting over any minute.

He couldn't get out of his mind that his political career was on the line tonight. For that matter, he thought, the Chief's career was also on the line.

And, another voice in the back of the mayor's mind reminded him that at this very moment, careers were of little importance to the 500 people in the theater.

12:35 A.M.

ESCAPE ROUTE (CHASE BEGINS)

Inside the theater, one man had yet to receive his share of the money. As Tonto stepped into the projection room, Jesse James turned and nodded. Silently, he walked past the Indian, down the steps, and into the lobby. J.J., like a lost man in the desert, had found an oasis.

Jesse James leaned over the barrel, almost falling in. His grin spread from ear to ear. This was not a mirage. This was more money than he ever imagined he would see in a lifetime.

Reaching down, J.J. fondled the packets. He had found true love. From now on, the world was his.

Inside the theater, the credits were flashing across the screen. 500 people knew the end was about to begin.

Opposite the theater on Topanga Canyon Blvd., Julie's father was nervously pacing. A trail of cigarette butts marked his path.

When Jesse James completed counting and pocketing his money, he carried the barrel into the men's room. There, he ripped a length of cloth towel from the wall rack and carefully wiped clean the plastic container.

When J.J. was satisfied, no telltale prints remained; he wiped it down again. They'd come a long way; they'd gone too far. Risked too much. No way was he going to become careless. Not now. Not when they were only three outs away from the perfect game.

Finally, sure that it was wiped clean, J.J. pushed the green barrel into the corner near the sink. He walked out of the john and back into the theater. The beginning of the first movie was being shown again.

Because they were running slightly behind schedule, the Lone Ranger had ordered the projectionist to again begin the second picture. L.R. had hoped this would take the edge off. It hadn't.

They needed only another 10 or 15 minutes. Maybe less. Their last role inside the theater was to change from their costumes to street clothes. It was the most difficult part of the operation, the trickiest. It had to be carried out with meticulous care.

If someone observed any of them changing, there was the possibility of identification later.

In spite of their agreement, the Lone Ranger promised himself that anybody who might see them changing would be a dead man.

L.R. pushed the walkie-talkie button. Jesse acknowledged the call. L.R. directed the uniform switch to be handled in the reverse order in which the money had been divvied up. J.J. was the first to change. As J.J. put the walkie-talkie back in his pocket, he scanned the aisle seats. In less than a minute, J.J. found what he was looking for. Briskly walking up the aisle, Jesse stopped and pointed his finger at a fat elderly man with thinning grey hair, seated one in from the aisle. Before Jesse could say anything, the man's face turned pale. His lower lip began to quiver.

Jesse James reached down and grabbed him by the arm. J.J. pulled him across the lap of the young girl seated on the aisle. As he tried to steady the old man, Jesse groped for reassuring words. He knew none.

Jesse put his arm on the man's shoulder. He led him slowly up the aisle, whispering reassuringly, "It's okay. You're not going to be hurt. I promise you. Just do as you're told. You'll be back in your seat in a couple of minutes." Jesse couldn't tell whether the words had registered.

They were past the double doors in the lobby, walking toward the men's room. "Are you all right?" Jesse asked.

The old man shook his head. He started to speak, but the words died in the old man's throat. Jesse led the old man into the first stall. "Face the door," he said. "Just stand there." Jesse walked back to the sink and sat on it, talking to the old man's back. "Listen to me carefully. But don't turn around. The most important thing for you to keep in mind is that no matter what, under no circumstances are you to look at my face. If you won't be able to identify me," Jesse said slowly, deliberately, "you will not be harmed."

"The only way you'll be in any danger is if you make the mistake of looking at me. Understand? If you want to get out of here, don't turn around. Don't look at me. Is that clear?"

The old man nodded his head.

"Okay. I'm going to go into a stall and shut the door. When you hear the door shut, turn around. I'll take off the costume I'm wearing and slide it under the door. You're to put on the costume. Put on everything I slide under the door. If the sleeves or the pants are too long, roll up the cuffs. Do whatever you have to do. Just make sure you get everything on. When you've got everything on—and this is extremely important—do exactly as I tell you."

"I'm still going to have my mask on," J.J. said. "Remember, you must never see my face. Therefore, it's important that when you have everything on, you stand with your back to the stalls. Don't turn around. When I tell you, and only when I tell you, I want you to turn toward the Men's Room door and walk straight to it. Take fifteen steps, and stop." J.J. hoped that that was clear. He didn't want the old guy to foul up.

"At that point, I'll come out. I'll get close behind you, and we'll both walk back to your seat. You'll sit down as if nothing happened. And that'll be it. Any questions?"

Getting no response, J.J. assumed his instructions were understood. "Fine," Jesse said. "I'm going to walk to your right side. When I tell you to, I want you to make a quarter turn slowly to your left. When I tell you, another quarter turn so that you end up facing the opposite direction of where you're facing now. Then, take half a dozen steps forward."

Jesse left the sink and stood up. He started to walk toward

the old man's right. "Okay," he said easily. "Make the first slow turn to your left."

Jesse watched. The old man had understood. J.J. kept walking.

When he was on the side of the stall, he called to the old man. "Make that second turn now." The old man did. "Now the half-dozen steps forward." Again, the old man obeyed. "Fine," Jesse said, relieved. "Stand right there."

Jesse didn't take his eyes off the old guy. He walked toward the stall door. "You're doing great," Jesse encouraged. "Keep it up." He stepped inside the cubicle and shut and locked the door.

Quickly, he stripped off the Jesse James costume, except the mask. He shoved the costume under the door, sat down on the john, and reached for his cigarettes. As he took a long, deep drag, J.J. called to the old man. "You can turn around now. Pick up the costume. I want you to put it on. Just the way I told you. When you're all dressed, let me know."

Jesse leaned his head against the marble wall and took another drag. He closed his eyes, once more savoring his share of the take. He tried to decide what he'd buy first.

1:05 A.M.

AFTERSHOCK (BODIES AND DUST)

As the screen began repeating the first flick, Don Pearson looked at his four daughters. Debbie and Linda were asleep. Tina and Tracy appeared drowsy. Don looked at the neighbours' kids. Two of them were asleep. The third was engrossed in the movie.

Don looked at June. Her head was erect, eyes staring at the screen. But Don knew that fear was raging within her. He wanted to take her in his arms and hold her reassuringly. Kiss her. Touch her. He couldn't. He had to sit still. Sit still and wait.

Somewhere in the back of his mind, Don was aware of a door slamming. He bowed his head and prayed.

Nancy glanced at Mac on her right. Without having to tell him, he'd know it was over. No matter what the outcome of this situation, Nancy's mind was firm. She was going to give her marriage another chance.

Nancy's thoughts suddenly centered on her husband. At that very moment, Tony might be outside the theater, planning desperately for the safe release of the hostages, unknowingly planning to save her life. Nancy surmised that Tony's Special Squad of Police must be one of the police teams at the scene.

"God," Nancy said very softly, squeezing her eyes tightly shut. "God, let me live."

John Ruffington sat very still. His hand was on the armrest, atop his girlfriend's. He patted her hand reassuringly. Acting as defense, prosecution, judge, and jury, John Ruffington reached a verdict.

John decided the cold facts entitled no one to condemn him. He was not guilty. He had tried but failed. He had, in fact, risked his own life, with the odds hopelessly stacked against him.

John finally had come to realize that he was a man... not a machine. No matter what happened now, John knew that Officer John Ruffington had distinguished himself in the face of danger. Nobody could put him down.

Julie looked at Bryan. She smiled understandingly. She didn't feel like a young adolescent any longer. She reached for Bryan's hand, took it, and squeezed it. She looked at Bryan in the dim light and tried to reassure him. Bryan looked back and smiled. He leaned close and whispered softly, "I'd like to take you out again if it's alright. Maybe to dinner and a movie."

1:11 A.M.

THE DEBRIEF (POLICE HQ)

In the parking lot outside the Mountain Theater, a dull quiet hung in the air. Several thousand people stared at the brick building with the glass front. They seemed to be awaiting a signal. And in a sense, they were awaiting a signal. In a sense, that signal would signify the beginning of a race. A life-and-death race.

1:12 A.M.

SMOKE CLEARS (AFTERMATH)

Tony Dangerfield stood between Mayor Lincoln Franklin and his boss, Chief Ray Boston.

The mayor looked at the buses dubiously. They were all in position. The buses formed a huge rectangle around the exit doors. Once the doors opened—if the doors opened—the hostages would spill out into the parking lot. According to the plan, hopefully, most of them would end up inside the buses.

While the hostages attempted to find their way to freedom, Tony Dangerfield's special team of police, along with the SWAT team, would try to identify the kidnappers. If the kidnappers boarded the buses, they'd have to contend with the bus driver, an expert marksman. If they made it past him, there were two more police sharpshooters aboard the bus.

It wasn't what Mayor Franklin would call good, but even the mayor had to admit, it was their only bet.

1:13 A.M.

FACES IN THE CROWD (PUBLIC REACTION)

Chief Ray Boston felt the tension inside his belly. He looked at his watch.

"Something's wrong," he said to Tony and the mayor. "They should have let the hostages out by now."

"Relax," Tony said. "We brought in a lot of money." He looked quickly at the mayor. "I imagine," he said sarcastically, "it must take a while to divvy up two million bucks."

The Chief searched his mind for something to say. He wanted to avoid any of this, particularly now. "Where's your STOP Squad?" the Chief asked instead.

"We already went through that," Tony said, annoyed. "They're going to be under the buses. They'll be out of the way. There's no way for them to be spotted by anyone. When enough of the hostages are out, they'll come out and get lost in the crowd. Their job is to spot the kidnappers. Once they've spotted them, they'll take them out."

The Chief nodded. "What kind of weapons are they carrying?"

"Handguns. Anything else, and they'd be too damn obvious," Tony explained. "Besides, I wouldn't dare let them use automatics in a crowd like that."

"How about clothing?" the mayor said. "Are they going to be

wearing anything that would distinguish them from the hostages? Or the kidnappers?"

Tony shook his head. "Soft clothes, period. Again, I had to avoid all risk of them being spotted. Our only hope is for them to get in and be with the crowd, unnoticed."

The mayor nodded. He looked first at Tony, then at the Chief. Then, in three words, he summed up the entire situation: "God help us!"

1:15 A.M.

DEBTS AND DEALS (PERSONAL COSTS)

Inside the theater sat 500 covered people. Six were convinced they were going to die. The six had been forced to change into the costumes worn by the kidnappers. Each tried to tell himself that it would be all alright. None believed it.

They knew they were being used to ensure the kidnappers escaped. Worse, they knew that if and when they were let out of the theater, the costumes would identify them as the kidnappers. They would probably be shot down on sight.

"L.R. to T,"

The Lone Ranger pushed a button on the walkie-talkie. "L.R.

"T. to L.R. Go."

"All systems go?" L.R. asked.

"Check," T. said.

"10-4."

"L.R. to W.B.H."

"W.B.H. Go, L.R."

"What's the word?"

"All's gone," W.B.H. said.

"10-4. L.R. to M."

"Go," the voice said.

"Are you set?" the Lone Ranger asked.

"Ready, willing, and able," Maverick responded.

"10-4. L.R. to J.J."

Jesse James reached into his sports jacket for his walkie-talkie. He pushed the talk button. "J.J. here. Go, L.R."

"We're ready at this end," the Lone Ranger said. "How about you?"

The silence was broken by the voice of the Lone Ranger.

"L.R. to J.J."

"J.J. Go."

"Begin final phase one," L.R. said.

"Check," Jesse James said.

500 pairs of eyes followed Jesse James down the aisle to the exit doors. J.J. stopped at the first set of doors, reached into his jacket, and took out a ring of keys. He fumbled with the keys. Finding the right one, he unsnapped one of the locks. Then he found a second key. Before unsnapping the second lock, he checked to make sure that everyone was still seated and that the team was in position.

A slip-up now could be disastrous. They were almost there. A few short minutes and they'd be home free. $2,000,000 free. Jess unsnapped the second lock. Slowly, quietly, he slid the heavy link chain out of the door handles.

At the same time, Tonto completed the same maneuver at the

other set of exit doors. Both sets of exit doors could now be easily opened from either inside or outside.

The Lone Ranger held the walkie-talkie tightly. He looked up at the screen. The picture was on. Nobody was watching. All eyes were on Tonto and Jesse James.

"J.J. to L.R.," a voice said into the walkie-talkie. "Phase one complete."

"Tonto to L.R. - Ditto."

"10-4," the Lone Ranger responded. "Back to your positions."

The Lone Ranger watched as Tonto and Jesse James walked up the aisle. He waited until they were in position. "L.R. to the team," L.R. said into the walkie-talkie. "We are now ready to begin the final stage. Remember the rehearsals. Keep cool. Remember your directions. Most of all, remember your treat."

1:22 A.M.

TRUTH REVEALED (LOOSE ENDS)

Individual jobs collectively complete a chain. If one screwed up, that link would break. And with it, the whole chain would fall.

The men manning the aisles closest to the doors started to lead people toward the exits.

Meanwhile, to keep order in the theater, the Lone Ranger addressed the crowd. "Please," he began. "Do exactly as you're told. Do it quickly and quietly, and you will not be harmed. As we promised you, once we have the money, you will be freed."

"Please follow the instructions of my men. As they tell you to move for the exit doors, do it quietly and quickly."

The Lone Ranger continued to repeat these instructions. His men continued to herd people toward the exits. The men nearest the exit doors watched the patrons spill out into the parking lot.

All hell started to break loose outside the theater as the crowd saw the hostages start streaming out. Behind the barricades, despite the police, people were trampling one another trying to get closer.

On the street, sirens screamed as emergency teams from as far away as North Hollywood raced toward the theater. Inside the rectangle, created by the buses, was a more peaceful scene.

Hundreds exited the theatre and were pouring into the rectangle. They were doing it quickly, orderly, and uncertainly.

Tony Dangerfield, on top of a bus, had a bullhorn in hand. He stood on the white roof and raised the bullhorn.

"Your attention, please," he barked into the bullhorn.

"Your attention. Please listen carefully. Do only as I tell you. I repeat, do only as I tell you. Get into the nearest bus. I repeat, climb into the nearest bus, and lie flat on the floor beneath a seat. Stay clear of the windows. There are enough buses for everybody. Climb into the nearest bus, and get to the floor."

As if students in a fire drill, most cooperated, quickly and quietly. They were scared, unsure, and looking for direction. Tony gave them that direction.

Behind the buses, crowds of people were running wild. TV cameras were being smashed; police barricades were crushed. Policemen, not wanting to use weapons, proved useless. They backed off. The crowd was given free rein in the parking area.

Inside the theater, people continued filing toward the exits, forming a continuous stream into the parking area. Four of the six costumed hostages were already in the lot.

Unknown to the four, telescopic rifles were already aimed at them from the roof of the theater. More guns were trained on them from the roofs of buses.

Standing atop the bus, Tony Dangerfield continued to bark orders. Most still continued to follow his instructions. The stream of hostages was subsiding. Tony gave the order for the first two buses to move out.

The engines couldn't be heard above the roar of the crowd. Within seconds, the two buses moved enough for waiting policemen to get inside the rectangle. Then the other buses moved back into position, closing the gap and keeping the crowd out.

As the second bus moved into position, six costumed men leaned spread-eagled against the buses. Three dozen uniformed and plainclothes cops covered them. Tony Dangerfield's Special Squad of Police patted them down.

As each Stop Squad member completed his search, each suspect was cuffed, hands behind his back, and led off to waiting police cars.

Four and a half minutes later, six innocent men were rushed into the West Valley Police Station.

It took four and a half hours of concentrated police effort to clean up and clear out the Mountain Theater parking area.

It took 35 minutes for Tony Dangerfield, Mayor Lincoln Franklin, and Chief Ray Boston to realize that they had messed up royally. As much as they didn't want to believe it, the men in custody had not been part of the kidnapping.

At that moment, Chief Ray Boston took command. He gave the order to search inside the theater. Then he walked to the parking area to check with other police on the buses. With everybody still in custody, the kidnappers had to be on the buses, in the rectangle, or in the theater.

Nobody, as far as Chief Boston knew, had penetrated the makeshift barricade.

Tony Dangerfield led a methodical search of the theater. Chief Ray Boston supervised his men as they interrogated the victims on the buses. It was a painstaking process. It could also prove dangerous.

It proved fruitless. It took Dangerfield's men an hour to satisfy themselves that the theater was empty. Names and IDs of all people on buses were taken. Finally, three hours and forty-three minutes after the first hostage had been "freed," Chief Boston released everybody.

Forty minutes later, scores of cops met in the Squad Room at the West Valley Station. At the podium stood three officials.

5:55 A.M.

DAWN AFTER THE HEIST (TONY REFLECTS)

Leaning with his elbows on the podium was Mayor Franklin. Flanking the mayor were Chief Ray Boston and Tony Dangerfield.

The mayor stared into the crowd. He held up his hands for silence. Dangerfield waited for the explosion. He knew the mayor was going to get even.

Tony knew the mayor would have to blame Tony. Hell, it was the mayor's career. As far as Tony was concerned, it was a fair exchange. All was fair in love and war. And he and his men had just won the war.

$285,714.28 apiece to be exact!

It was theirs. They'd gotten away with it.

Mayor Franklin could do all the screaming he wanted to. Tony's STOP SQUAD had the last laugh. The joke was on Mayor Lincoln Franklin. They were a Special Team of Police.

Tony looked at the mayor. He didn't want to miss a word.

"Gentlemen," Mayor Franklin began. "First of all, let me commend you on the fine job you did under the worst of conditions."

The mayor looked squarely at Tony. "You did what was paramount in everybody's mind—you protected the lives of

500 innocent people. Furthermore, you did so without firing a single shot. And, on top of all this, you carried it off without costing the city one thin dime."

There was a restless buzzing in the room. Tony shifted from foot to foot. What the hell was he talking about?

The mayor again held up his hand for silence. "If you will recall," the mayor continued, "When this thing broke, I was up North. Most of you will remember the recent raid staged by San Francisco police and Federal agents who confiscated several million dollars in counterfeit money. They were, I might add, damned good counterfeits. But not quite good enough."

"Yes, the two-million-dollar ransom demand was met. The payoff was made with $2,000,000 of that counterfeit money."

"I want to especially thank Tony Dangerfield and his Special Team of Police," the mayor concluded.

THE FOLLOWING TUESDAY

TRICK OR TREAT REDUX

The following Tuesday night, several men sat around a poker table. They were Tony Dangerfield and his Special Team of Police... a.k.a. Maverick, Wild Bill Hickok, Tonto, Jesse James, the Lone Ranger, and Roy Rogers.

They were playing no-limit poker for chips. Next to the poker table stood a green plastic barrel. Inside that trash receptacle lay $2,000,000 in counterfeit money.

www.ingramcontent.com/pod-product-compliance
Lightning Source LLC
Chambersburg PA
CBHW071843211125
35704CB00008B/277
9798349618567